SATAN

MW01286998

"Clements hits all the right notes... but he especially shines in the sailing detail. Solid noir, worthy of a new life."

—Bill Ott, *Booklist*

"If you like a salty, dark adventure mystery, just hop on board this ship. Not many good people sail in this story. Mrs. Sloan is your *femme fatale*, Lewandowski is full of culpable behavior, and together they weave a devious scheme. Throw in the dark ship, exotic ports and the emotional games between the two characters, and we have a fine crime noir story."

—August West, *Vintage Hardboiled Reads*

"If you like a book with *fatale* attraction, murder and mayhem, and a protagonist that isn't much better than the "temptress," than track down a copy of this book."

—Frank Loose

Satan Takes the Helm

by Calvin Clements

Black Gat Books • Eureka California

SATAN TAKES THE HELM

Published by Black Gat Books
A division of Stark House Press
1315 H Street
Eureka, CA 95501, USA
griffinskye3@sbcglobal.net
www.starkhousepress.com

SATAN TAKES THE HELM
Originally published in paperback by Gold Medal Books, New
York, and copyright © 1952 by Fawcett Publications Inc.

ISBN-13: 978-1-951473-14-3

Book design by Jeff Vorzimmer, *¡caliente!Design*, Austin, Texas
Proofreading by Bill Kelly
Cover art by Barye Phillips from the original edition.

First Stark House Press/Black Gat Edition: October 2020

Chapter One

You didn't need government statistics or a business bulletin or any of that stuff. Not in my business you didn't.

You saw for yourself the idle freighters tied up, their sides red with rust, the silent wharves and the loneliness of the harbors. In shipping you saw jammed hiring halls with proud masters asking for mate berths, mates asking for anything and expecting nothing, willing to work the fo'c'sle where they started from. You walked around and saw these things and a thousand faces with the same so-goddamn-tired-of-it expression. The jokers with the fat cigars had said this year would be better, and in one way they were right. With a little money you could buy anything.

Now I mean anything.

Like the time you stood on the corner of the Embarcadero and Market and the tall redheaded kid with the timid blue eyes watched you for a half hour before she got up the nerve to ask if you wanted a good time, mister. First it was a beauty contest in Godknowswhere, Kansas, then Hollywood at twelve bucks a day for too few days, then looking for a job, any job, then do you want a good time, mister. You were young and looked pretty decent and she was more shy and embarrassed than frightened, but it wasn't a good time. It was a lousy time and she cried a lot but she got her buck and next time maybe it would be easier.

Everybody still scratching for a buck. That's the way it was.

It was that way here, in San Francisco, two months after I was paid off the Balsco. It was July and hot and the morning mist was rolling back off the water front. Groups of jobless seamen were beginning to crowd the Embarcadero, loitering along the foot of the piers, looking up at the freighters and tankers, studying the rat guards. Like at a wake, just standing around and looking, in twos and threes, maybe fifty to a block.

A streetcar made its U turn at the foot of Market and a few more got off to join them. Garrett was one of them. He spotted me on the corner where I'd given an industrious boozer the job of shining my shoes.

"Lewandowski, that you?" Garrett came over, walking slowly, his nearsighted eyes squinting against the morning sun. The lines in his stubbled face had deepened but he looked about the same.

"Pull up a chair, Pappy, and watch the parade. Hey, do you have to spit on that shoe?"

The boozer grinned up at me, unveiling naked gums stained with tobacco juice. "Makes 'em slicker, Cap. Holds the shine better."

"I'll settle for a straight polish job. What's new, Pappy?"

Garrett shrugged. He stood beside me, hands thrust in the pockets of his uniform coat, his faded eyes blinking over at the aimless wanderings of the jobless. "How long is it going to last, Martin?"

"Forever, Pappy. How long has it been with you?"

"Two years. Two rotten years. If it was just me, all right, the hell with it. But five kids and one on the way." He shook his head.

"Self-control, Pappy. When you're on the beach like this you've got to practice self-control."

It was a crumby joke. He didn't crack a smile. He placed a finger against his nostril, leaned out over the curb, and neatly blew his nose. "And they don't even care about us, Martin. That's the hell of it. Went up to Red Star this morning to see Kruger. Figured after two years on the beach he'd see his way clear to find a spot for me, even watchman on the stuff he has tied up. Couldn't get past the girl at the desk."

"Dead-pan Mary still guarding the portals?"

"The same. Tried to explain to her I had thirty years with the company and maybe Kruger would place me somewhere, or if he didn't have anything then he'd sort of keep me in mind after seeing me, refresh his memory I'm still around. She just sat there, scraping her nails. Not a blessed thing to do but she couldn't get out of that chair to ask Kruger about it. Said it'd be a waste of effort."

His seamy face took on a scowl. "Imagine it, Martin. Couldn't get up to walk twenty feet to that door. And Kruger sitting up there on his fat behind and can't even take the time to see a man who works thirty years for him. They're all like that. They've had the fat years and socked it away, and now they don't give a damn for anybody."

Garrett was sore. He wasn't a radical, a commie. Just sore. A guy with five kids. So he had a right to be sore.

I dropped a quarter into the boozer's outstretched hand. "Let's cry in a few beers, Pappy. I'm buying."

We went across the street to the Anchor and stood at the bar and we had a beer. In a booth in the rear two noisy sailors were arguing the merits of subs versus destroyers. A bored stringy blonde sat between them fingering an empty glass. We had another beer and Garrett pulled a crumpled scrap of paper from his pocket and smoothed it out on the bar. "The Brentwood, Room 5B."

"Got this as a tip from Solly last night. You know Sol Golden? Well, he answered an ad in the Examiner calling for a chief officer holding a full top ticket. It gave just a box number and asked for a letter giving qualifications and things like that. Solly wrote one out and got a reply with this address. He didn't get the job so he passed it along to me for a try."

"I take it you didn't make out?"

He shook his head, reached for a pretzel. "I was stopped by the room clerk. It's one of those small places where you have to have a room or phone up to see if you're expected before you can get by the lobby. Managed to talk to some woman over the phone, getting in a word about thirty years' experience and so on, but she said I'd be too old anyway."

"When you pass fifty, Pappy, you're supposed to blow your brains out, or didn't you know? What outfit was doing the hiring?"

"Never did find out, but if they're hiring from a hotel room, somebody's rigging a ship with a cheap crew. That's the way I figure it."

That would be the score, all right. One of the lines putting a vessel in service but wanting no part of the regular men, the old-timers trying to fill time for a pension and others maybe getting full-scale wages. It happens a lot. A freighter, say, operates out of Seattle. So they send her down to Frisco and one of the office secretaries of the line, working from a hotel room, advertises for a crew. They get one, dirt cheap. When the ship shows in Seattle the regulars squawk, but it was an emergency, see, and what do you want the company to do, fire these poor bastards after just hiring them?

"You might try for it, Martin—unless you're still on the Balsco payroll?"

"She's a dead pigeon for a while, Pappy, but this other thing's probably filled ten times over."

We had another beer. The sailors had shifted the argument to torpedoes versus depth bombs. They were really having a high time. The blonde chippy had her elbows on the table, chin cupped in hands, staring up at the ceiling. I picked up the scrap of paper from the bar, folded it lengthwise, creased wings along the sides the way the kids in school do, and sailed it down the length of the bar.

The chippy gave me a tired smile.

"Try it anyway, Martin. If you get past the clerk you might get an interview without a letter."

"Solly's a good man, Pappy. He muffed the job with an invite, so where do I fit in?"

"Maybe Solly's appearance didn't suit the woman doing the hiring."

"And mine might? Thanks, Pappy."

He shrugged. "Females are funny sometimes when it comes to figuring the best man for a job. That fancy Balsco uniform you're wearing might go over, Martin."

In the long mirror behind the bar my blue uniform did look pretty impressive with the four gold stripes on each sleeve and the gold-braided cap, but the outfit was not even remotely related to the Balsco. This one was a special from Fineberg's Tailoring, All Garments Fitted and Guaranteed, and it set me back $92.50. Ordinarily, window dressing doesn't mean much when a skipper makes the rounds looking for a berth, but with me it did. I mean I needed something to offset a thick Polack face with a standing five-o'clock shadow and a nose that had been broken twice and looked it; with me it was a flashy front or risk being taken for a Hunkie just off a banana pier after a hard day.

"Another beer, Pappy?"

He shook his head. "I'll be getting over to the hiring hall, see if anything's come up."

I handed a five-dollar bill to the barkeep. He made the change and put four-forty on the bar.

"Pick it up, Pappy."

He looked at the money and rubbed his unshaven chin. "Be a long time getting it back, Martin."

"So it'll be a long time."

I left him at the corner of Market, and took a cab uptown to the Brentwood. The doorman standing under the green canopy was in full dress. He showed me his teeth and swung open the hotel door.

"What's that fellow's name at the desk again?"

"Frisbee, Captain. Milton Frisbee."

The small lobby was dimly lighted, the usual red-carpeted lounge with soft chairs and potted palms. A single elevator faced the desk. The wispy clerk stopped talking to a colored bellhop to peer at me over his glasses. He started to open his mouth when I stepped into the elevator but I beat him to the punch.

"Say, Frisbee, will you look into the hot-water situation? My shower ran cold last night."

He gave me a courteous smile, as a good desk clerk should. "I'll look into the matter immediately, sir."

While he was still trying to figure out who I was and when I had checked in, I got off at the fifth floor and walked down the hall to 5B. I knocked on the door and waited and knocked again. Behind the door somebody said something and when I opened it I realized she must have said anything except come in.

She was just in the act of picking up a pink robe from the foot of the bed, a tall brunette with dark hair piled in a bun behind a pale cameo face. She was bending forward, one hand reaching for the robe, her head turned to the door, mouth opened in surprise, wearing nothing but a sheer bra and panties. For a frozen moment she gaped at me, then grabbed the robe, slipping one arm through a sleeve, getting tangled up with the other and forgetting to turn her back, giving me a front view of high bold breasts fighting the restraining brassiere. It was quite a show while she fumbled with that other sleeve.

She finally drew the robe about her, tying it, glaring over at me. She wasn't pretty; her mouth was too thin and her skin too sallow. There were faint shadows under her eyes. She looked thirty and frustrated.

"When you're through looking, you might explain

the meaning of barging in like this!" Her voice was like ice.

"I knocked—"

"I heard you! I said to wait a moment!"

"I'm sorry. I thought you said to come in. My name is Lewandowski. Martin Lewandowski. After I sent you the letter I thought—"

"What letter are you talking about?"

"In answer to the ad you put in the Examiner. After sending the letter I thought—"

"I received no letter from you! A name like yours I wouldn't be apt to forget so soon." Her eyes were a pale frosty green, cold and level. She looked like a woman who had both feet on the ground and was acquainted with most of the answers.

"It *is* quite a name." I stepped into the room and closed the door behind me. Her eyes hardened. "Quite a name, all right. People are always pulling the old chestnut do you spell or whistle it. I always figured it might be better to get some cards printed, but it's something you just never get around to."

"Let's get back to the letter. I didn't get it. If I did, I know I didn't answer it. And just how did you know this address when I used a box number?"

"Friend of mine received a reply from you. Name of Sol Golden. You probably recall talking to him. Anyway, we both sent inquiries a few days ago, and when he got a reply from you and I didn't, we figured my letter was lost in the mail." I spread my hands out. "So he gave me this address and suggested I come up to see you."

Her frosty eyes traveled over my uniform. "Perhaps I had no wish to interview you. There were many letters I made no reply to."

"My qualifications were about the same as Solly's. We figured if you answered one, you would answer the other."

"Do you always lie with such a straight face? You

never sent any such letter!"

She had both feet on the ground, all right. "O.K., so I didn't send a letter. No letter, no interview. Is that it?"

"That's quite correct. Now if you don't mind leaving, I'll finish with my dressing."

"It'd take me just one minute flat to give you my qualifications and then you could say no and I'd leave feeling that I at least had a chance at the job. Happy ending, sort of."

Her eyes flicked over my uniform again. "I'm sorry, Captain, but ..."

She studied my face. Whatever she saw there took a few seconds to think about. Then she turned and walked over to a night table beside the bed, came up with a cigarette and lit it. Smoke curled from her mouth up into her nostrils as she motioned to a deep chair across the room.

"Sit there. What did you say your name was?"

"Martin Lewandowski." I was looking over at the bed, at an opened traveling bag with some clothes folded beside it. If she were packing to leave, it seemed reasonable to assume her job was finished here, the berth filled.

I was mulling that one over when she took a small pad and pencil from a handbag and motioned to the chair again.

"I said you may sit down."

I went over and sat down, my cap in my lap, its gold trimmings facing her way.

"What's your background, Captain Lewandowski? Briefly, if you please." She half sat, half leaned on the edge of the night table, pad in one hand, pencil in the other, her cool eyes appraising the cap. She didn't seem too impressed.

"All told, seven years under license, six of them in mate capacities, the last year as skipper of the Balsco."

"Let's start further back. What did you do before going to sea?"

"Nothing that would be of interest to a shipowner."

"Suppose you let me decide that. I haven't much time, so just mention the type of work and the reason for leaving."

"O.K. There wasn't much schooling. I started in the coal mines when I was sixteen. Couldn't see it. Too much sweat for three meals a day. Tried a lumber camp for a while, but that worked out pretty much the same. Muscle men eat but they don't get rich. I was a flop at selling vacuum cleaners, and the same with Fuller brushes. Just not the type that gets past the door."

"And then?"

She had shifted her feet, the folds of the robe parting above her knees. She had thin legs but curvy. Nice.

"And *then*, Captain Lewandowski?"

"On the road a while. Bumming. Some fighting in Chicago. In the ring, I mean. That's where I got this nose. Decided it wasn't worth the damage and came on to the Coast."

I lit a cigarette while she wrote something on the pad. I couldn't figure the line of questioning. The first thing a hiring agent wants to know is length of service in the various grades held, and class of vessels served on. That's important. Anything else is pretty irrelevant, since the government checks for a criminal record or anything like that before issuing the original license as merchant-marine officer. What counts after being licensed is whether you've spent your time on tanker, freighter, or passenger and how long, and that's the type of question I figured she should be asking if she knew her business.

I had the feeling she did know her business, so it was that much more puzzling.

"And what have you done on the Coast?"

She moved away from the night table and sat down on the bed, drawing the robe close as she crossed her legs. She supported the pad on her knee. Somewhere in a room above us a woman giggled.

"Odd jobs. Marking time. Dishwashing, bellhop, attendant at a drive-in, a one-day extra's bit at Warner's."

She looked over at me.

"It was a college-boy shot. Hard to believe, but true."

"There's nothing wrong with your face, if that's what you mean. You have a strong face. Different."

"That's the kindest thing that's ever been said about it."

"What happened after the movie career?"

"Got talked into shipping out on a tanker. It was O.K. but I couldn't see much point in remaining an A.B. The boys wearing the stripes on their sleeves were getting the dough, what there was of it. The boys on the bottom were getting it, period."

"So you decided to get the stripes on your sleeves?"

"A few books stood in the way, a few years of decking. But I made up my mind to get a master's ticket."

"You made up your mind?"

"At the time it seemed a handy thing to have, something you could fall back on."

She clicked the pencil against her teeth. They were nice teeth, white and even. "You make up your mind to get something and that's all there is to it?"

"Just like you." The words were out before I gave them a second thought, but that's exactly the way she impressed me, a woman who knew just where she was going, the length of the trip, and the fare to the penny.

She gave me a quick look and went back to the

pad. "How old are you?"

"Thirty-one."

"You look older."

"Maybe I've lived longer."

"Married?"

"Never in one place long enough to get that well acquainted."

She frowned and bit on her lower lip, leaning forward slightly, as if studying the pad, the robe opening and forming a long V at the throat. You could see the curve of her full breasts rising above the brassiere.

I got up, looking for an ash tray. There was one on the table by the bed. I moved over to it, bent down, and rubbed the cigarette out, my head maybe six inches from hers. I was beginning to enjoy the close-up when the pad caught my eye.

There wasn't a damn thing on it except a bunch of circles and crosses.

O.K., we were playing games. The job was taken. If she was seriously considering me as a possibility, she'd be writing down the facts to send along to her boss. Maybe she liked interviewing guys down on their luck. There are some like that, some that get a kick out of playing big shot to the poor slobs looking for work.

She looked up at me warily, as if on the defensive, her lips parted slightly. It was an impulse, perhaps to take her down a peg, or maybe I figured I had nothing to lose. I leaned over and kissed her, hard. It was so-so.

She regarded me calmly. "What gave you the idea you could do that?"

I sat down beside her. "Let me ask the questions for a change. Why this runaround? Your bag is being packed and you're leaving here, right? So why these questions when you've got a guy picked for the job?"

She drew some circles on the pad. "It's true that I

have already hired someone, but I could always change my mind."

"Why should you change it?"

She changed to crosses. "Perhaps you fit the bill better. This job calls for someone young and a bit hard-boiled, someone who wouldn't be too squeamish about cutting expenses to the bone—and a little beyond when called for. I presume you know what I mean when I say a little beyond?"

I knew what she meant, all right. Most vessels stick close to government regulations in the matter of food for the crew, their working hours, decent quarters with periodic fumigation, and things like that. Now, toeing the line on these items costs money. Big money. And when you have a vessel going all out to save a dime, really going all out, I mean, and say the vessel carries a crew of thirty—well, you have twenty-nine miserable hands. The thirtieth, the skipper, is making a very nice penny on a percentage basis and his sole worry is to keep one step ahead of the marine inspectors while he and the owner are pocketing the dough.

"I can go along with any policy, but I thought you were looking for a chief officer. The skipper is the boy with the whip hand in those matters."

"You've heard of the Eastern Trader?"

The Eastern Trader was a tramp freighter, free-lancing between the West Coast and Asiatic ports. She was owned and operated by Ezra Sloan, an old-time sailing captain who was reputed to be pretty soft to work for. I had seen Sloan only once, limping up a pier, and vaguely remembered him as being crippled and having some sort of facial disfigurement that was not too pleasant to look at.

I said I'd heard of the Trader, also of Sloan.

"Your position will be that of chief officer aboard her, but you'll be expected to run the ship, taking complete charge. For some time Captain Sloan has been too ill to take much part in the handling of his vessel and you'll have a free hand. Salary will be one hundred and fifteen a month, plus ten per cent of the net, paid quarterly."

It sounded fishy. The 10 per cent, I mean. Too high.

"A hundred and fifteen a month doesn't interest me. Ten per cent does. But that's double the going rate for skippers working on percentage, so I gather the net of the Trader is zero."

She nodded. "Close to it."

"I'm to build it up?"

"That's correct. You are making your own berth."

"O.K., that's all right. I don't mind starting from scratch. The question is what happens if I build that net up to where it means something to me? I know some owners who would cut the ten to five and then to three. The idea being the better you do, the less the percentage."

She shook her head and closed the pad. "Captain Sloan has settled on ten per cent as the worth of a capable master who will relieve him of all duties, and he has no intentions of reneging. His reputation for dealing fairly with everyone is well known, so you needn't have any worries on that score."

It was beginning to sound good.

"Which brings up another question. After a certain point, saving a buck on a freighter means taking it out of someone's hide, in one form if not another. Will Sloan, if he levels all around, go along with that kind of saving? What I mean is, I don't care to be working for peanuts and that's what I'd be getting if I'm stuck with a squaredeal-all-around-and-happy-ship setup."

"It has been rather like that, but it's going to change. Captain Sloan no longer has much choice in the matter. His capital is low, and once the vessel runs at a loss he'll have to tie it up. I said you would have a free hand and you will." She looked annoyed. "My, I thought you'd be jumping at this job."

"I like to have things straight. I'm not exactly broke, so I can be a little choosy for a while. The job is mine, then?"

"Your papers in order?"

"I have them here." From my inside pocket I took a large envelope containing my license and a half-dozen references. She went through them slowly.

Her robe was still partly opened, enough for me to become absorbed in the silent battle going on behind the filmy flesh-colored brassiere she wore. It was a lace affair, and each time she breathed I expected something to pop. What might happen if she took a deep breath was beginning to fascinate me when she handed my papers back.

"I'm sure these will satisfy Captain Sloan."

"The job is mine? I mean you have the last word on this?"

"It has been left entirely in my hands."

"Listen, how about buying you a dinner tonight? Show my appreciation."

She shook her head, reached for her handbag, and put the pad and pencil away. "I'll be busy tonight."

"This other guy you hired? What about him?"

"I'll notify him the deal is off."

"Slip him a couple of weeks' pay and charge it to my salary."

She snapped the bag closed and looked at me half quizzically. "I didn't think you were the sentimental type."

"Two weeks' salary won't break me. Maybe the guy has a wife and seven kids."

She made a face. "My God, seven kids. What a thought to wish on the poor man."

"Kids are all right."

"But not seven."

"When am I going to see you again?" I put my

arm behind her, resting it on the bed.

"Who said you were?" She arched her brow in a side glance. Her green eyes were slanted a bit at the corners, her skin faintly freckled and not as sallow as I'd thought.

I put my arm lightly around her waist. All she had to do was draw away or stand up and it would be O.K. I'd play it her way. No harm done. But she didn't draw away or stand up. She fiddled with the strap on the handbag. An engraved invitation.

"*Will* I see you again?"

"Perhaps."

She turned her head as I pulled her close, clinging a little when I kissed her, moving her mouth against mine. She had a clean outdoor smell. The belt holding the robe together was tied with a simple overhand knot. It came loose without my half trying.

"Lewandowski, stop that. Who told you— Stop that, I said."

It didn't sound very convincing. Not after that kiss. Maybe she wanted more preliminaries.

"You're pretty nice."

"Lewandowski, will you—"

"Martin."

"Well, Martin, then, but take your hand away."

"You don't want me to." And she didn't. Her cheeks were flushed, her green eyes turning smoky. Quick, sure, but an old story with the cold and strictly business type. One close smell of a man and *wham*, they were gone.

"Martin, listen ... Listen ... *Will you listen?*"

"I'm listening."

"Not now."

"When?"

"Later."

"How much later?"

"Will you please stop acting like an animal?"

"How much later?"

"You'll see me plenty of times."

"Don't hand me that. The Trader is out of this port eleven months out of twelve. What's wrong with now?"

She pushed me away suddenly and stood up. "Because I'm due aboard the Trader before noon. There's a number of things I have to do before we sail."

I stared up at her. "Before *we* sail?"

She drew the robe about her and pushed back a stray hair. "I'm Mrs. Ezra Sloan. I share my husband's cabin aboard."

She smiled at my expression. "I'll dress in the bathroom, so if you care to wait here we can go down to the Trader together."

It was only a half-dozen steps to that bathroom door, but before she had reached it my mind was made up that the "later" stuff would be out. The Eastern Trader at $115 and 10 per cent was a nice deal and it might turn into just the type of berth I'd been waiting for, a permanent well-paying niche in the shipping business. There was nothing permanent in a setup involving the boss's wife, so it would be all business from here on in.

"By the way, Martin ..." She paused with her hand on the door, looking back over her shoulder. "My husband is quite sensitive about his appearance. His face is badly scarred, as you probably know, and he becomes moody for days afterward if anyone avoids looking at his face while talking to him. I thought I'd mention it."

"Good thing to know, Mrs. Sloan. Thanks for the tip."

"He uses a cane to get about, but don't ever take his arm. Best to ignore it, even when he's in difficulty."

"I'll remember."

"And the name is Joyce, Martin."

It took me a split second to think that one over. "Happy to know you, Mrs. Sloan."

Her eyebrows rose slightly. She smiled. "I believe I'll be quite happy to know you, too, Martin."

Chapter Two

"I think you'll like it aboard the Trader, Mr. Lewandowski. We don't stand much on ceremony between hands or officers, and we try to make it a home for both." A sharp-boned, wasted man in his seventies, Sloan bent his bald head over the log on his desk, his veiny hand trembling as he guided the pen through the entry.

Behind Sloan stood his wife, her hands resting on his stooped shoulders, smiling over at me, looking cool and fresh in a gray skirt and white silk blouse open at the throat. You had a tough time keeping your eyes off the blouse, partly because of the buttons, which were shaped like pearls and looked real, and partly because of the sheerness of the silk.

She was one baby well aware of what she carried and didn't mind drawing attention to it.

"I hope these terms are satisfactory, Mr. Lewandowski. The salary is small and I'm afraid your percentage will not net you very much for a while."

"I'm completely satisfied, sir, to tie my earnings in with those of the Eastern Trader."

He nodded without looking up. "Good. Good. I'm glad to hear you're considering it in that light. The long-range view, it's been my experience, is generally the best." His pen continued scratching away.

Despite his wife's reminder, it had been somewhat of a shock seeing Sloan again, for I'd forgotten just how badly he was disfigured. Sloan's sunken cheeks were masses of scar tissue where the pox had once taken hold. The deeply pitted skin was an ugly thing to look at, but it was the knife slash that made you want to look elsewhere. It started under his right eye, a broad purple-gray welt twisting down alongside his nose to the corner of his wrinkled mouth, where his lower lip hung loose and protruding, as if here the nerve had been severed. The combined effect, the sagging lip and the raised scar leading directly to it, was as if something unpleasant was constantly seeping from his eye down into his waiting mouth. He'd really taken a beating in his time.

"With a woman aboard a working freighter, Mr. Lewandowski, you might think you have to dress or act somewhat differently than you're accustomed to, but it isn't so." Sloan raised his head from the log. His eyes, set deep in wrinkled sockets, were a surprising soft clear blue and you had the feeling a small child was peering at you from behind a grotesque Halloween mask.

"I never aim to have my comfort at the crew's expense. Of course, we might watch our language a little and things like that."

"I understand."

He put the pen in its holder, reached back, and gently pressed his wife's hand, which was still resting on his shoulder. "Love, we might offer Mr. Lewandowski refreshments. Suppose we break out some of that new brandy. You do drink brandy, Mr. Lewandowski?"

"Brandy will be fine."

While she busied herself at the dining table, setting out decanter and glasses, Sloan settled back in his chair and idly leafed through my papers. My eyes strayed to the side door leading to an adjoining stateroom. The door was partly ajar and I caught sight of twin bunks, neatly made, well separated by a wide night table. For some reason I was relieved to see they did not sleep together. None of my business, but there you are.

"Ever ship under sail, Mr. Lewandowski?"

"That would be quite a bit before my time, sir."

He nodded thoughtfully. "True. For the moment I forgot your age. A few lumber schooners are still around, but that's about all." He put the papers down and sighed. "Those were better days, Mr. Lewandowski—suppose I call you Martin—better days by far, Martin. Everything was slower then. Gave a man a chance to think. Seems to me money wasn't so important then, either." His thin hand lifted to indicate the interior of the cabin. "A sign of old age, they say, but I find it comforting at times to hold on a little to the old days."

He was holding on more than a little, for the cabin was a replica of the sailing-era cabins. It was a small room, long and narrow, with a low false-beamed ceiling and bulkhead walls paneled in dark teakwood. The floor was covered with a yellow fiber rug that had apparently been made in one of the islands, and all the furnishings, the hand-carved buffet, chairs, Sloan's desk, and the long dining table, were of the same heavy bleached oak you seldom see around. In the center of the room, over the dining table, swung a brass hurricane lamp, another sailing-day touch.

Sloan started to get up, reaching for a cane by his side. "It's all right, Martin. I can manage."

He managed, but it was quite a job. His right leg was a trifle shorter than his left and he winced as he slowly limped over to the table. Joyce held a chair back and he sank into it gratefully, smiling up at her.

She frowned as she handed him a glass with a small amount of brandy. "I don't know why you insist on getting about with that cane when you actually need a wheelchair. You're being very foolish, Ezra. I think I'll go ahead and order one whether you like it or not."

He wagged a bony finger at her. "You'll do no such thing, love. I appreciate the thought behind it, but when the time comes a mariner can't stand on his own legs, wobbly or not, he doesn't belong on a working freighter." He lifted his glass and tilted it in my direction. "Here's to better days for ships and the men that run them."

We drank the toast. Sloan set his glass down, a wry expression puckering his wrinkled lips. "Never could stand this stuff. Keep it for guests." He settled back in his chair. "Before we go any further, Martin, let's talk a little about me." He looked at me, his brow lifting. "I'm far from nice-looking. Do we have any trouble agreeing on that point?"

What was there to say? Yes? No?

"I see we're agreed. So let's add these bad features up. You've noticed the leg? Well, I got that in a Singapore bar. As innocent bystanders so often do, I got the worst of the scrap that broke out. Sixteen I was at the time, just standing there and talking, when this chair comes flying across the room, catching me across the shinbone. In those days bone infections were more fatal than not, so I guess you can say I was lucky." He shifted in his chair. "Lately, it's been painful putting my weight on it. Bone deterioration, they say. Been advised to have it off, but the little time I have left I'd sort of like to keep me in one piece."

He gently touched his scarred mouth. "Same year it was I got this. Walking down the wharf one night and jumped by a Malayan. Probably mistook me for someone else, but it didn't make the results any different after he finished with that knife." He gazed for a moment at his glass, as if lost in thought. "The pox came from rounding the Horn before I was twenty-one. There were twenty in the crew and to the man they came down with it. I managed to survive, along with three others, but when I saw in a mirror what had been added to the knife scar, it was a long time before I could convince myself it would have been better not to."

"Pretty tough all around."

He straightened in the chair, rousing himself. "Martin, I'm not telling you this because I'm looking for sympathy. It's simply when you continually have to be around a man like me, somebody as ugly as the devil, it might help if you understood how it all came about, sort of removing the mystery, you might say. Then, too, after we've talked about it like this, I figure a man won't be so apt to look past my shoulder when talking to me. That's embarrassing both to him and to me."

He smiled across at me, a grotesque expression because only one side of his mouth moved. "So, Martin, we'll say I'm as ugly as sin but it doesn't bother me none—not now, it doesn't—and we'll both forget about it. Now let's get down to business. Joyce has told you you'll be in complete charge, assuming the duties of the master. There'll be no interference from me, unless I figure you don't know your business—and I gather you do from the nice things the Balsco people say in your reference."

The reference should have been good. I had been working cheap enough. "By complete charge you mean O.K.'ing the buying of stores, hiring and firing, things like that?"

He rubbed his bony chin thoughtfully. "Well, I hope there'll be little need for firing anybody, Martin. It's a cruel thing these days to set a man on the beach if we can hold him on."

A warning glance from Joyce stopped me from pressing this subject. The one thing she had emphasized on our way from the hotel was the saving of the dollar with no holds barred, and she would take care of any objection from Sloan on the cutting of the crew if I saw fit to do so.

"But you'll be the boss, Martin, because I intend to confine my activities to owner and agent, more or less. Incidentally, I've logged you as master, not chief officer. It'll give you the run of things without anybody questioning your authority or trying to go over your head to me."

I nodded my thanks. An hour aboard and logged as master. This was turning out to be a berth.

"I'm a little ashamed to admit you'll find much to be done, Martin. During the past two years I've been getting around less and less and I'm sure many things could stand improvement. At first, I had considered moving Phelps up from second mate to chief officer, but Joyce seemed to think he's not too good a businessman." He smiled across at Joyce, who was filling my glass again. "My doll baby is pretty much the boss around here."

She raised her head and smiled right back at him, but I saw something in that smile apparently Sloan did not. I mean it required plenty of effort to look him straight in the face. A young woman marries a man like Sloan for just one reason, and I knew right then she was sweating out every dollar she was getting or hoped to get when he died.

"You'll find, Martin, the crew is well paid and a happy lot, and I'd rather leave it so. Mind you, I'm not tying your hands. The time may come when a small temporary cut may be necessary if we're to keep operating. Let's just say we'll try not to hurt anybody and leave it at that."

We left it at that and there was some small shop talk, a straightening out the watches and so on. Joyce got together the log and some account books I would be needing, then offered to show me to my room.

It was located forward of the cabin, off the same passageway. The door to the room preceding it was opened and she stopped there to show me an office layout, desk, chair, a large safe, and a filing cabinet. Shelving around the walls held the usual slop-chest selections, dry goods, toilet articles, candy, stuff like that. In one corner stood two cases of liquor.

"This is *my* job; storekeeper, bookkeeper, and paymaster."

"Busy girl."

"Not too. If I didn't have a little something to do on these crossings I think I'd go crazy from boredom."

"Is that private stock?" I motioned to the liquor in the corner.

"Not at all. Help yourself, any time."

"You can charge a couple of bottles against me, then. The nightcap habit is hard to break."

"I like one occasionally, too, generally when the weather is rough. You're this way...."

It was a small room but neatly furnished, with the same teakwood paneling on the bulkhead walls as in the master's cabin. On one side was a maple bureau, a brass clock and barometer fixed above it; on the opposite side a well-filled bookcase took up most of the wall. Lending a homey effect was a deep leather chair and a floor lamp.

"Not too roomy, Martin, I know."

"Suits me fine."

She motioned to the large bunk suspended under the twin ports. "It's 'spring.' I guess you're happy to see that."

"You bet."

I walked over to inspect the framed painting hanging above the bunk. It was a clipper ship weathering a gale in with full canvas, picturesque as hell but lousy seamanship. You could see, too, it wasn't a professional job.

"Who's the artist?"

She came over and stood close to me. She had something on that smelled good. "That's Ezra's work. He dabbles a bit. You'll find his handiwork displayed in most of the staterooms. Take it down if you wish."

"Looks good. We'll leave it."

She asked for a cigarette. I lit up two and handed

her one.

"I'll have a desk brought in, Martin. You'll be needing that much, I know. If there's anything else you want, don't hesitate to mention it."

"Everything's fine. Never had it so good." I went over and tried out the leather chair. I felt right at home. It was a good berth, damned good. I owed Garrett a favor.

She put the log and ledgers she was carrying on the bunk and opened the ports, dogging them back. A warm breeze drifted into the room, along with a loud and profane argument going on between some longshoremen on the wharf outside. She grimaced as she turned away from the ports.

"Why men must use such words I'll never know."

"Rough territory, the water front. You have to live with the language a while before you stop noticing it."

"Six years married and on board is the answer to your question, Martin."

She smiled over at me with the smoke curling from her mouth up into her nostrils, a habit of hers I was becoming used to. "With that little feminine victory under my belt, suppose we discuss what suggestions of Ezra's—he'll give you no outright orders—you'll ignore. For one thing, you are to pay no attention to this nobody-gets-hurt idea of his. That policy has cost him money in the past and in these times we need to be more realistic. That's one reason I decided to hire a chief officer myself, one who could not only handle a ship but could be a little ruthless if it meant saving money."

"From Sloan's attitude I'd say he wasn't very interested in doing anything but break even. Maybe he's got a nice kitty put aside to draw on in case of a setback, so he's not worried."

She shook her head, moved over to the port, and flicked the ash from her cigarette. "There isn't a penny, except the few thousand we carry aboard for current needs. No bank account, and a lovely five-figure mortgage. That's what frightens me so. Ezra doesn't seem to realize that if business gets any worse we'll be forced to stop operating. In such an event it's not entirely inconceivable that we could lose the vessel."

"How stubborn will Sloan get if I try to do a job on personnel?"

"Don't you worry about Ezra's interfering. He's out of his cabin so seldom these days I doubt he would miss a single man if half the crew were suddenly changed. Anyway, I'll take care of any objections from him, *on any point*. I intend to run things here, Martin, so you'll have no one to answer to but me." She sat down on the bunk, crossing her legs and smoothing her skirt in one motion.

"You're quite a woman."

She looked up, her eyes shaded slightly. "I'm speaking of business, Martin, and I want you to pay close attention. None of your flippancy. I admire that free and easy manner, but only at the right time. What happens to this ship will mean a great deal to me."

I caught the inflection on the "will." "I meant it as a compliment, but go ahead. I'm listening."

"After you go through some of those accounts, I'm sure you'll find expenses that can be eliminated. There's simply no excuse for running without a profit—not when Ezra has such fine contacts here and in Asia. We've cut rates, of course, to meet competition, but there's still no reason why we can't show a profit. I'll leave it up to you to cut where you can. Don't hesitate to make any changes if it means a dollar in our pockets."

"Don't worry. I'll hold up my end."

"You're not going to get much help from either Phelps or Ferguson, I can tell you that. Both

Ferguson—he's the chief engineer—and Phelps have reached the age where they don't seem to care for changes, content more or less to go along in their own plodding way. I suppose it's Ezra's fault they believe business as usual will keep us going. He pats them on the back, says things are great, they're wonderful, and keep up the good work. And that attitude is costing us plenty, believe me. Our expenses are a good third above the expenses of other freighters of comparable size. I know because I've been checking on it."

"I'll take care of Phelps and Ferguson."

She shook her head. "You won't be able to fire them, if that's what you mean. That's one thing Ezra would immediately overrule you on, any of his officers leaving."

"I'll wake them up. If I let a hand go do I send him to you or Sloan?"

"Send him to me. I handle the payroll, so you needn't upset Ezra with anything like that. He'd hem and haw and it would wind up with the man staying aboard. Do anything you wish, Martin, if it means our financial condition will improve. Our expenses must be cut, somehow, in some manner. If they aren't ..." She studied the end of her cigarette. "I'll fire you, Martin. As fast as I hired you I'll fire you and hire another man."

I didn't doubt her for one minute. Money matters would be the first order of business here. "O.K., the ship gets turned upside down. You just keep Sloan off my neck."

"I said I'd take care of him. He's so busy nursing that leg these days he'll be glad to stay out of the way. You don't know how relieved he is now that he's handing his duties over to someone else."

"He's really quite a guy. I mean, after you get kicked in the teeth as often as he did, you're apt to be a little grouchy. He seems to have an even disposition."

She shrugged. "He's easy to get along with."

I didn't ask the reason why she married Sloan, because a quarter-million-dollar freighter is a pretty good reason for doing almost anything.

"I think that's about all, Martin." She took a deep drag from the cigarette, got up, and tossed it out the port.

She came over to my chair and lowered herself onto my lap. "Surprised?"

"Well, yes."

"I don't think you are, Martin. Not really. We're pretty much alike, you and I. You know: being direct and all that."

"Best way to be, I guess." The quick switch from business to pleasure had thrown me into a mental fog.

"Like me, Martin?"

"Sure I do."

"I'd feel like a complete ninny if you said you didn't." She traced the line of my jaw with her fingertips. "Well, Martin?"

"Well, what?"

"You weren't so reluctant to show it this morning. That you liked me, I mean."

"I didn't know you were married then."

"That part really worry you?"

"Not ordinarily, but this would be a little different."

"Why different?"

Her fingertips trembled as they played along my lips. Her expression was calm enough but you could sense the want building up in her, the fire she was trying to conceal.

You couldn't help but wonder what it would be like.

"Well, after seeing him like he is, can't get around and so on, you think about him. I mean he's a pretty good skate and it sort of makes the difference. No?"

She put her mouth against mine, gently, her arms

sliding behind my neck. The points of her hard breasts pushed against me as she tightened her arms.

"Listen ... Joyce ..."

Her moist lips began teasing.

The hell with Sloan. This one time, anyway.

"These look like real pearls."

"They *are* real. I have three more just like them. Careful. They unbutton easily enough."

Sure enough, they did.

"Couldn't help but be a little curious about this thing this morning."

"Curious?" She rested her head on my shoulder, her breath quick and warm on my neck. "In what way, Martin?"

"Well, there's no straps and it doesn't look very strong, Looks as if it couldn't give without tearing. Yet it does."

"It was made specially for me in Hong Kong, darling. There's elastic woven in with the lace. If you rip it I'll make you buy me a new one."

"It'd be worth it."

"There's a little hook in the back." She got to her feet, holding her unbuttoned blouse together, leaving the thin piece of silk in my hands.

She turned and walked unsteadily over to the bunk. She was really gone.

"Bring me a cigarette, Martin."

"You don't want a cigarette." I left the bra on the chair and went over and stood over her. She was still holding the blouse together, not trying to button it, her eyes lowered.

"I feel like a common hussy, Martin."

"We can cut this short and forget it, blame it on the weather."

She didn't say anything. She lifted her eyes. They were glassy. She sank back on the bunk and stared at me a moment. Then her hands left the blouse and she put them behind her head and the blouse spread open, sliding down the side of each breast.

On deck a winch groaned. It stopped groaning. It hummed. Something crashed on the wharf outside and a longshoreman loosened a string of curses. The room was warm, her skin moist. "Martin ..."

"Yes?"

"Darling ... Oh, darling ..."

"Lower your voice. Someone will hear you."

"I don't care who hears me. Darling. My sweet, sweet—"

I clamped my hand over her mouth. She squirmed and bit it, hard. I swore and pulled it away.

"Martin, I love you!"

"I love you, too, but listen—"

"I mean it, Martin. I love you."

"Joyce, you've got to be more quiet. They'll hear you." I hated talkers.

"I feel like screaming."

"Good God—"

"I won't. I just feel like it. Martin, darling, do you love me? *Really*, I mean?"

"Sure I do." My hand ached from her teeth.

"Everything will work out fine, Martin. You don't know how glad I am you're aboard, darling. Oh, darling—"

I clamped my hand over her mouth again. She didn't bite this time. If she had I'd have socked her right on the jaw.

Chapter Three

We were sailing at midnight. I helped supervise the loading, and by six the holds were filled and hatches battened down, the winches secured and booms cradled.

With the wharf gang off the ship I took a quick tour of it to get my bearings and saw something that made me wonder if Sloan was half blind as well as crippled. Standing on the wharf and looking up at the Trader you saw a long, sleek, black-hulled freighter of six thousand tons with its long booms and squat stack in spotless buff. You saw a freshly enameled bridge house gleaming with a coat of white porcelain and the after deckhouse the same. From the wharf you saw it that way and you'd say neat as a pin but you'd be wrong. Dead wrong. Close up she was scabby. I mean you could pick at that nice shiny paint in almost any spot with your fingernail and come up with a quarter-inch rust scab. Maybe that means nothing to you. You might say they were saving money at a time when money was tight. On the surface that was so, but only on the surface. Actually, they weren't saving a dime.

In the first place, the paint slapped over that rust costs money, and you have to keep slapping it on twice as thick to conceal the rust and twice as often as over healthy metal. Secondly, a reckoning was due and you couldn't get away from it. That rust keeps eating into good steel, and the day would come when borings would show certain plates needed replacing and then the shipyard bills would be large enough to wipe out a year's profits. Maybe there aren't any profits to wipe out. O.K., you're out of business. And I don't mean this was something that could happen to the Trader in the far-off future. Hull inspections come once a year, and when the inspectors gauged the metal as too thin, that would be it. I'd be back on the beach, my hat in my hand.

Sloan ran a happy ship, all right. From what I saw the crew stood watches and swung an occasional paintbrush and everybody was satisfied a job was being done, including the officers. O.K., it would be changed and there was only one way to do it. Phelps and Ferguson were the key men, and unless I wanted to beat my brains out each day overseeing the doings of twenty men, these were the two babies to straighten out, but fast.

I wondered just how sore I could get Engineer Ferguson and Mate Phelps.

We'd see.

Ferguson was testing the engine throttle when I came down the ladder. He was a tall dour-faced Scotsman wearing a walrus mustache and oil-stained coveralls. A stubby corncob hung from his yellowed teeth.

"I'm Lewandowski. Taking over for Sloan."

He removed the pipe from his mouth, his small eyes turning cautious. "So I heard. Glad to have you aboard."

But he wasn't glad. He had been getting along fine under the old setup. Nobody likes to change a good thing.

I ruffled the sheaf of job order copies I held in my hand. They were almost a year old, dating from the Trader's previous trip to the yard.

"I've been reading through this stuff, Ferguson. About fifty per cent of it could have been done aboard, I figured. Perhaps more."

He scratched a leathery cheek with the pipestem, giving me the patronizing smile reserved for deck officers foolish enough to question engine-room work.

"A big difference the goings-on below decks than up in that chartroom, Captain. Nobody expects you to know what could or couldn't be done aboard."

"Stow it, Ferguson! I don't have to sleep with this stuff to know what makes it tick. Here are items for rebricking donkey boiler, a hundred and fifty dollars; retubing lubricating oil cooler, eleven hundred and twenty-five; a compressor and water-pump overhaul job at a hundred and five. Don't tell me those jobs couldn't have been done aboard, because I happen to know better. Give, and make it good."

His mustache drooped as his smile faded. He jabbed the pipe at my chest. "I don't like the way you question my job, young fellow!"

I pushed the pipe aside. "The title is Captain, the name is Lewandowski. Use them in the future. Now let's get something straightened out right here. What'll you bet I can't go topside, get your pay envelope and a reference from Sloan, and see that you don't trip over the gangway getting off?"

It was a bluff on my part. He didn't call it. He stood there sizing me up, wondering how far I could go, if Sloan would back me up.

I tapped the papers in my hands. "O.K., let's try it again. On your recommendation this work was let out for bid. Why wasn't it done aboard?"

He studied the bowl of his pipe, then the stem. He rubbed the stem against his coveralls. "Seems to me you're reading off major repairs?"

"Considered so, yes."

"Well, I don't say some of them couldn't be done aboard, but the usual thing is to wait until we get into the yard."

"O.K., this stuff is water under the bridge so we'll forget it. But after this the usual thing will be to do this kind of work aboard." I motioned to a bunch of rags lying between the main cylinders. "What are those doing down there?"

The patronizing smile came back. "Why, to catch the leaking oil, of course."

"I know they're catching oil. I also know the price of that oil is eighty dollars a barrel. Why hasn't the condition been remedied?"

The smile disappeared. "It will be, next week, when we get to the yard in San Pedro."

"Is that all you can think of when something goes wrong, the yard? Did it occur to you it could be fixed right here?"

He spat his disgust, jammed the pipe in his mouth,

and rocked back on his heels. "Now you're telling me we can install cylinder base gaskets aboard?"

"That's exactly what I'm telling you, because I've seen it done by a live-wire chief. It's a hell of a job, sure, but it can be done. The next port we lay over in, you lift those cylinders and get them installed. And listen, Ferguson, any work that must go to the yards, O.K., but if it can possibly be done by your men I'll expect you to do it. Tools I'll get for you, but in the future if I find work slated for outside that a good chief can do aboard, we'll find a good chief to do it. Tie that one on tight, Ferguson, because I mean business!"

His long dour face was turning a brick red, but he kept his lips clamped around the pipe. I walked around on the floor plates a minute, frowning at the machinery, whether I understood its operation or not. Ordinarily, a skipper leaves his engine room alone, and I wanted to plant a get-it-fixed-before-that-sonofabitch-Lewandowski-sees-it impression so I could do just that. There'd be enough worries topside without my hopping below each day to see if a buck was being saved where it could be.

I started to go up the ladder when I noticed two burly wipers on the catwalk above.

"You have nine in your gang, including yourself, right?"

He barely nodded, his eyes on a pressure gauge that wasn't even registering. He was sore, all right.

"Well, you can do with six. Get rid of the two wipers and one assistant. Your oilers can double as wipers."

His head snapped around. "Our papers call for nine."

"I know what our papers call for. Get rid of those men before we shove off. Send them to Mrs. Sloan for their pay. Which assistant to get rid of I'll leave up to you. Keep your best men."

"You're leaving me with two assistants to stand watches?"

"That's right."

He didn't get it. "I need three assistants. Four on and eight off they're working."

"You make the third."

He got it. The pipe almost fell from his mouth. "You expect me to stand watches?"

"You haven't forgotten how, have you?"

His mustache actually quivered. "Twenty years I've been sailing with the old man. Twenty years as chief."

"So you have. So what? You've been well treated and what have you done in return? Nothing. If you were on the ball and had a little gratitude for the steady berth, some of that red ink in Sloan's books might be black. In the past year alone over six thousand went for yard labor in this engine room, labor that was on our payroll and should've been used. Wake up, Ferguson. The picnic is over."

I left him sputtering for an answer and went topside, around to the galley. The cook was a fat moon-faced Filipino named Silva and called Laughing Boy by the crew. While we had been loading I gathered from the crew's remarks he was quite a character, not exactly crazy, more happy than anything else. I understood he had a habit of sneaking up behind seamen when they were bending over and holding about two inches from their behinds a six-inch clasp knife that snapped open by the touch of a spring. After pressing the spring he'd go into hysterics at the results.

Just a happy boy.

He was standing over a meat block, two hundred pounds of blubber in filthy whites, the clasp knife in his hand, opened, the tip of the blade held between his thumb and forefinger. I thought he was playing mumblety-peg on the meat block until I saw the black cockroach weaving across the scarred wood. It was a big roach, fat and lazy, its movements slow.

Silva's broad lips parted into a gold-toothed grin as I stepped into the galley. He kept his eyes on the roach, which was nearing the end of the block.

"Captain Lewandowski! Good evening to you, sir, coffee? A bit of cake? Perhaps a salami sandwich? There's cold"—the knife spun, the blade smashing into the meat block a fraction of an inch from the head of the startled roach—"beer in the refrigerator."

"How much kickback have you been getting from the chandlers on this grub?"

His tiny black eyes, almost hidden behind their fleshy lids, followed the roach retracing its steps. He pulled the knife free. "Now, Captain, you know I wouldn't—"

"The hell you wouldn't. You're no different from any of these other hash-slingers afloat when the buying is left up to them. How much is the kickback?"

He kept giving me the gold-tooth treatment. "Well, they"—the knife spun again in a silver arc, the roach halting in front of the quivering blade—"do remember me at times, Captain, sir. Just a little, though, you understand."

"I'll bet it's just a little! At eighty-four cents a day per man it's a damn sight more than a little. Starting today I want that cut to fifty cents. And I don't mean you're to throw slops on the tables. I can snap my fingers and get a dozen cooks that can make like Thanksgiving on fifty cents."

His dark head bobbed merrily in agreement. He pulled the knife free again, the roach moving off at a right angle. "Can't lose by trying it, Captain! We'll certainly try it. Never know until we try something. Fifty cents a man it is." The roach suddenly came to life, scurrying to the edge of the block and down the side. Silva giggled and wiped the blade of the knife across his greasy coat.

He wasn't crazy. Not much.

"And if I ever see another roach in this place, Silva, I'll personally stuff it and see that you make a meal of it."

He ha-ha'd with all teeth flashing, bending over and slapping his knee. "Anything you say, Captain! You're the boss! You say it, I do it."

Forward on the well deck, three of the hands were rolling dice on a blanket spread between the winches. Over by the starboard rail, near the gangway, two others, a skinny Cuban and a heavy-faced Italian, were gabbing to two girls on the dock. I went over to the rail.

"You two men grab a broom and give these decks a sweep-down. Mop that water out of the gutter while you're at it."

They looked at me blankly. You'd have thought I ordered them to jump over the side.

The Italian scratched himself. "All through for today, Cap." He looked at the Cuban. "No, José?"

José stopped picking his nose long enough to nod agreement.

"You're through, all right. Both of you." I jerked my thumb forward. "Go up and get your pay."

Panic crept over the Italian's face. "Geeze, Cap, what'd I say?" He turned to José, who was looking pained. "What'd I say, José, what'd I say?" He flung his arms in the air. "What'd I say, Cap, what'd I—"

"You're not asked to say! You just do as you're told. Now hop to it with that broom and next time don't question orders."

The crap game had broken up fast. Two of the men were hurrying forward to help with the sweep-down. The third, a tall blond kid in a sweat-stained T shirt, was trying to push a wad of bills into his pocket and fold the blanket at the same time. I called him over.

"What's your name?"

He looked scared. "Gerlack, sir."

I pointed to the line on the forward bitts, some thirty feet of which had been pushed haphazardly into the gutter.

"Fake that line properly."

"I didn't leave it like that, Captain."

"I didn't ask if you did. I said fake it down. And the next time I catch a man ignoring anything as sloppy as that I'll toss him right on the beach and no questions asked."

I walked away. It was petty stuff, sure, but the less seamen have to do, the less they expect to do. These boys would be more than earning their pay from now on and I wanted them to get used to the idea right from the start. Save a lot of breath later on.

I sent for Phelps and was behind the flat-top desk that had been moved to my room when he walked in. He was a big-waisted man wearing double-lensed glasses that gave him an owlish, uncertain expression. I'd seen some slow-moving and slow-thinking men in my time, but Phelps topped them all if his loading directions a few hours before had been a sample of his work.

He stood in front of my desk looking more uncertain than usual, as if he had been talking to Ferguson and had an idea of what was coming.

"Phelps, I've decided to cancel this yard bid. We'll bypass Pedro and go straight to Diego. Now I see that you made this survey, so maybe you can tell me what it's all about. Take this item: water tanks scaled and cemented, two hundred and seventy-five dollars. Here's another: anchor chain overhauled, one hundred and sixty-eight." I read off a half-dozen more, then sat back and looked up at him. "How come?"

He removed his glasses and fumbled with them, frowning as if he were mulling over some deep problem. He put his glasses on and adjusted them. "How come what?"

"How come it isn't being done by our hands?"

He made a vague gesture. "They just don't do that sort of thing."

"Starting today, they do. In the future our own hands will do all overhauling with the exception of the bottom and the masts." I pulled out another bit sheet. "Fantail railing, thirty-four feet to be replaced at seventeen dollars a foot. I thought we carried a carpenter."

He looked surprised, then smiled. "Surely you don't expect him to replace railing?"

"If he can't do it, we'll get someone who can."

"But to shape a fantail railing—"

"For God's sake, Phelps, I've known carpenters to shape railing with an adz! If this man doesn't know his business we'll replace him. That applies to anyone aboard." I wondered if Phelps was as touchy as Ferguson. "Including you!"

He blinked down at me. Slowly he straightened his shoulders, cleared his throat, started to speak, and then changed his mind. He removed his glasses, wiped them with a handkerchief, and replaced them. He cleared his throat again. Finally he got it out.

"I don't like to be talked to that way, Lewandowski."

"Captain Lewandowski. And I'll tell you what I told Ferguson. The gangway's down. Use it. Get your things and blow if you can't take it."

He cleared his throat again. "You can't fire me."

"Want to make an issue of that point?"

"I've been with Ezra since he bought this vessel. I've been—"

"You too, eh? The one big happy family routine. Well, that's finished, Phelps. Things are being changed and if you can't go along with them you're not needed aboard. Now, let's get back to the business at hand. Who's been painting over rust and why hasn't it been scaled?"

I waited until he went through the routine with the glasses again. "Haven't the money for scaling. And there isn't much else you can do but paint over it. It would look terrible if you didn't."

"After this let it look terrible. There'll be no painting over rust. You talk about money for scaling and I assume you mean a yard job. Don't we carry scaling hammers aboard?"

He looked shocked. "We do, but surely you don't expect the men to scale the ship?"

"I expect them to do what they can. From now on I want the deck gang busy on that project, from nine to five. Start them aft, on the deck. When we reach Shanghai we'll take on a coolie gang for the bulkheads and sides, and each time we run the coast we can get a good piece of it done. You can have this ship scaled from the water line to the bridge within six months for slops and petty cash. It should have been done long ago."

I held out the bid sheets for the deck work. "Put a couple of good men on this exclusively. Follow it up and see that it's done before we return to the States."

He took the sheets and hesitated. "Seems to me you're asking a lot of work from a deck force of eleven."

"Eight, not eleven. Get rid of three before we sail. Send them to Mrs. Sloan for their money."

"Only eight men—"

I opened the log, a little tired of Second Mate Phelps. "I'm busy, Phelps. You have your orders."

He didn't leave. He stood there fidgeting with the bid sheets.

"Something on your mind?"

"Well, we're due for a fumigation. It was listed with the yard work in Pedro."

"We'll get around to it some other time."

He hesitated. "There's been droppings noticed. Even found forward in the crew's compartment."

"If you're squeamish about a few rats, Phelps, get a box of rat-chaser for your room."

He stared at me indignantly. "That stuff smells to high heaven!"

"Which goes to show we can't have everything, doesn't it?"

He closed the door a little harder than necessary when he went out, surprising me. I didn't think he had it in him.

I found Weber, the third mate, on the bridge, working in the chartroom. He was just twenty-one, a chinless, sandy-haired kid with a pink pimpled face. He snapped to attention when I walked in, and for a moment I thought he was going to salute me. He caught himself just in time. "Weber, I understand you started here in the fo'c'sle. Had the brains to hit the books?"

"That's right, sir." He tried to look modest.

"Sloan endorsed your application for license and gave you your first opening. You owe him a lot, don't you?"

He beamed. "I certainly do, sir. He put me on that first rung and I'm not forgetting it."

"Just how far will you go to pay Sloan back?"

His forehead wrinkled. "Why … Well, I don't know, sir. Do just about anything for the old man, I guess."

"Would you resign?"

He looked at me as if I were crazy. "Resign! Well … gosh … gee, I—"

"Here's how it shapes up, Weber. We're going on the rocks, financially, I mean. Sloan is worried sick how to make ends meet and stay clear of the receivers. Now you know how he is about firing anybody. Just can't bring himself to do it. Well, he's down there in his cabin now, his mind pretty much made up he should stand your watches to save the money but not able to bring himself to pass you the word. He talked about how fond of you he was, and how he's going to hate to put you on the beach. Understand now, I'm not telling you to quit. I'm just stating the facts, knowing you'd want to go along with anything Sloan has in mind. I know he's not feeling so good and it would be a load off his mind if you relieved him of the job of telling you—assuming he *could* bring himself around to it. Seems to me, Weber, as long as he gave you your start, it'd be a nice way to pay him back."

He looked sick. "Gee, I never thought it was that bad."

I slapped him on the shoulder. "Hell, man, you came aboard a deck hand and you're leaving a licensed officer! You're sitting on top of the world. Listen, here's a tip: Don't go in the cabin looking so glum when you say good-by. You'll make Sloan feel bad. Then again, he'd know I had spoken to you about this and might feel I was butting into his affairs. Tell him you've got a better berth ashore. Sure, that's it. Then he can give you the usual sorry-to-see-you-go and everybody will be feeling fine. And don't think I won't be keeping you in mind at the first opening, or if things pick up. In fact, Weber, I'm going to make it a point to give you a push along the ladder sometime in the future. And maybe a lot sooner than you think."

He looked a bit more cheerful. "Fair enough."

I held out my hand. "Still friends?"

He gripped it and started pumping. "Hell, yes, Skipper! And listen, thanks for being so frank about this."

I spent the next few hours in my room, studying the past cargoes, gross profits, and previous expenses.

Killing time until Weber left. At nine he was off the ship and I went down the wharf and put in a call to Masters, Mates, and Pilots, leaving a message there for Garrett to report aboard the Trader as its third officer that evening, or to catch the ship at Diego, our next stop.

Joyce was busy in her storeroom office when I walked in. She looked worried.

"It's been like a parade in here, since this afternoon. On paper the money saved looks fine, but are you sure we won't run into trouble with the inspectors?"

I sat on the edge of the desk. "When the time comes for a ticket renewal we'll have a full crew—for that one month."

"Oh—I see."

"Even if you're caught, it's a slap on the wrist compared to the dough saved. I'll take care of things. What are we paying the A.B.s? Scale?"

"Slightly better. Fifty-three a month."

"O.K., we'll cut fifteen per cent, right up the line, starting today. In a month or two, when they stop griping, we'll slice them another ten."

She looked uncertain. "That much? I had thought of five, ten at the most."

"We may as well do it up brown, where it means something. Does Sloan know we're riding light yet?"

She shook her head. "Hasn't been out of the cabin all day. He's trying to rest that leg as much as possible. Generally it's at night that it bothers him the most, but today it seems to be acting up more than usual."

"Maybe he *should* have it off."

She grimaced. "Please, Martin, I'm the one that has to live with him. Besides, he doesn't believe in operations. He's a very religious man and has an almost fanatical belief that nothing should be done to alter the course of a person's life. Particularly surgery."

"The worse you do here, the better things will be in the hereafter?"

"Something like that. He has funny ideas about the dead, especially when it comes to seamen. Don't ever laugh at his notions. You can disagree, but don't laugh."

"When a man pays my salary I never laugh at him."

"I just want to bring you up to date on Ezra's ways so you'll get along with him well."

"We'll get along O.K. Listen, Weber is leaving the third berth open. I'm filling it with an old-timer named Garrett. Good man, Garrett. I've sailed with him a few times. All right with you?"

She looked up at me steadily. "Weber was very devoted to Ezra. Funny he should decide to leave just the day you come aboard."

"Another job, I believe."

"So *he* said."

"It's O.K. about Garrett, isn't it?"

She chewed on the end of the pencil, her green eyes thoughtful. "I want you to stop lying to me, Martin. You got rid of Weber to create an opening for a friend. Weber means nothing to me, so I'm willing to go along with you on this. Just don't lie to me about these things or you and I will be having trouble; there's nothing we can't agree on if we talk it out. Understand? Now lower that conniving face here and we'll make up."

Garrett arrived twenty minutes before we were ready to shove off. He came puffing up the gangway, a duffel bag over his shoulder, the sweat streaming down his weathered face.

"Martin, lad, couldn't believe it! Wonderful. Don't know how to thank you."

"Forget it, Pappy. This evens us up. There's an

empty on the port side. Any sleep today?"

"No, but that's all right."

"Get some, you're on at four. Things are pretty much squared away anyhow."

I went up to the bridge and was standing by in the starboard wing when Phelps reported the radio operator had not come aboard yet. For a moment I thought of cutting the payroll further, then dropped the idea. You can push the steamboat inspectors just so far.

"O.K., Phelps. We'll pick one up in Diego if he doesn't show."

He lifted his cap to scratch a patchily bald head. "Maybe I should mention Sandora's been with us a long time, Mr. Lew—Captain. He's probably liquored up again, but he's never more than ten or fifteen minutes late."

"Mean you've been in the habit of waiting for him?"

Phelps shrugged. "Ezra's pretty lenient with him."

"He *has* been lenient. Better get that gangway up. Midnight we'll be under way."

But we didn't get under way at midnight and Phelps hadn't time to raise the gangway. From the wheelhouse I heard hoarse shouting and the name Sandora, then a high-pitched screaming that was choked into silence almost as soon as it started.

I dropped the dividers and went out on the bridge, over to the railing. Below me, on the pier, two deck hands stood in the yellow glare of the cargo light, gaping at something under the gangway. They looked as if they wanted to go someplace and be sick, and when I saw what they were looking at I didn't blame them. All you could see of Sandora was his upturned white face, the blood spurting through his clenched teeth. The rest of his body was hidden, meshed between the side of the ship and the dock fender she rested against.

Freighter gangways aren't built to accommodate drunks, and it was pretty plain that Sandora had staggered up his last. He had apparently fallen at the same instant the vessel had momentarily swayed at the berth, six thousand dead-weight tons catching and clamping him against the fender.

I went down on the well deck where the hands were lining the rail, some gawking down, some turning away, unable to stomach the sight. Joyce came hurrying from the cabin struggling into a coat, Sloan limping behind her. They went over to the rail.

I sent Phelps to put a police call through, waited a few minutes for Sloan to get over the shock, then got him aside.

"Sir, there's not a thing we can do to help Sandora, and if we permit it this ship will be overrun by a dozen guys waving reports they'll want filled out."

"Poor devil."

"You can say that again, sir. Now I suggest rather than take chances on a twenty-four-hour delay, or even more if a couple of steamboat men decide to hold us up for a check, we drop a man off here to take care of things and then pick him up in Diego. We certainly can't help Sandora by running up some wharfage."

"Tragic case, Martin. His drinking came from a disturbed mind…. Oh, yes, yes, by all means. Take any action you see fit. You run the vessel as if I were ashore."

For the next thirty minutes I was busy filling out accident reports for the steamboat inspectors and trying to convince two cops you don't hold up a vessel from sailing simply because a drunk couldn't navigate the gangway, and besides, marine accidents came under federal jurisdiction.

One of the cops, a beefy guy with a pin-stripe suit that looked as if it'd been slept in, kept leaning over my desk and breathing in my face.

"Look, skipper, it ain't that we *like* taking something like this over. We got it *handed* to us. My boys just got finished scraping Sandora off that whatumacallit—"

"Fender, Lieutenant. And listen, that was sure a dirty job. Don't think I don't appreciate it. Say, behind you in that bureau is a bottle. Why don't you and your partner—No, top drawer. That's it."

By the time I finished the reports, the lieutenant—who turned out to be a sergeant and wouldn't go any higher because he'd told that brown-nosing ward heeler where to go and he'd tell 'im off again, just wait and see—decided he'd let the coroner worry about witnesses for the inquiry.

After they left I called Garrett in and handed him the reports. "We'll pick you up in Diego, Pappy. That bunch down at the bureau will be blowing their tops because I didn't phone and give them a chance to go crawling over the ship, but you feed them a line. Happened fast, just when we were pulling out, big contract in Diego and if we don't show ten thousand lost. Lay it on thick. But listen, first thing tonight get over to the Hall and send us a radio operator. Some cutie at the bureau will pick that up when you hand in the reports showing Sandora was the operator and maybe bag us in Diego if we shove off without one. And see if you can get a medical report on Sandora. He was loaded to the ears and it should show in writing. If it doesn't, make a beef. Some relatives might come looking for a piece of change and we can wave the medical report in front of them. You listening, Pappy?"

Garret had been fingering the reports, a faraway look in his eyes. "Sorry, Martin. I'll take care of things. I guess my mind was on that woman."

"Mrs. Sloan? What about her?"

"Oh, it's really nothing much. Just the way she

stood by on the dock when they were removing the body. She kept looking on so calmly, so composed, taking it all in."

"Some women are like that, Pappy. Plenty of stomach. Better hop to it, now, and don't forget about that operator. Try to get one over within an hour."

The operator came aboard a little after two o'clock, a tall gloomy guy with a hatchet nose. He stood at the head of the gangway looking around as if he was undecided.

"Something wrong?"

He looked over at me and got gloomier. "Don't like filling a dead man's shoes."

"Who does? But that gangway is coming up in ten seconds, so make up your mind."

He made it up and went below.

Thirty minutes later I was standing on the bridge, watching the distant shore lights receding, feeling for the first time in two months a deck vibrating under my feet. It was a good feeling, and I found it hard to realize that less than twenty hours before I had been standing on a corner with my hands in my pockets.

All in all, it had been quite a day.

Chapter Four

We put in to Diego at noon and took on a deck load of Fords. Garrett came aboard and told me the inspectors had thrown a fit because I hadn't given them a chance for an on-the-spot investigation. The first thing they had done was check on whether I'd got a new operator before sailing, then settled for a grumble at Garrett when they saw I'd kept one step ahead of them.

"They were just looking for something to do,

Pappy. I'll buy them a dinner and drinks when we get back and have them cooing over my shoulder."

That night, under way and headed west on the run to Shanghai, Sloan elected to do the eight-to-twelve watch and I went up on the bridge about eleven-thirty to relieve him.

He was standing out in the chilly darkness of the port wing, his face half buried in the heavy blue coat he wore. From his position, half leaning over the weatherboard, he seemed to be listening to something.

"Pretty cool night, sir. If you care to go below, I'll take over."

He didn't stir from the position. His eyes were half closed. I spoke again and he turned.

"Sorry, Martin. Been standing there long?"

"Just came up this minute. If you were feeling sleepy, sir, you could have sent the watch for me."

He shook his head. "Not asleep, Martin. Just listening to their whispers."

I glanced down over the rail, to the forward decks. Except for the dark shape of the lookout in the forepeak, there was no one about.

"Out there, Martin." Sloan tilted his head out at the dark sea surging by. "'Course, you're young yet, and there's few you've known that's been buried out there, so you're not likely to hear."

It took me a few seconds to get what he was driving at, to recall what Joyce had spoken about and connect the two. I lit a cigarette and played it deadpan.

"I say you're young, Martin, so you haven't heard. But you will in time. You will if you follow the sea long enough. You'll see many a man chuted over the side and you'll remember those men, and later, if you listen close enough when the ship has quieted, you'll hear them." He turned and smiled, as if a little embarrassed, the darkness softening the ugliness of his face. "But you don't believe me, Martin, do you?"

"Sorry, sir, but if you're speaking of the dead, I don't."

He shook his head slightly. "Not just any dead, Martin. Just the souls given to the sea for keeping. The ones you've known well and have sailed with. You may not believe it, but you can take my word there'll be a time when you'll hear them. Perhaps it only happens to those who are getting along in years and will soon be joining them. I don't know. But you can hear them, all right. When the wind is right you can hear their whispers."

Now I've heard the wind when it plays across the surface of the water, through the troughs, changing pitch when the swells spill and flatten, and maybe sometimes it sounds almost human. Sloan was not the first old-timer I heard claim the sound *was* human, but he was the first that claimed it who I thought was more than levelheaded.

"I'm an old man, Martin, and you might say I'm hearing things, but I'm not. I know I'm not because sometimes I can pick out the voices of those I've sailed with when I was a clipper cabin boy, some sixty years ago. I actually recognize those voices, and that's the reason I know it's not the wind brushing off the combers. Perhaps I shouldn't talk about it so much because a body's first reaction is that the Captain's becoming senile."

I was wishing he'd go below.

He was silent for a few moments, gazing into the night. I tossed the cigarette over the side and watched the flame arc into the white-lipped wash rushing astern.

"Another reason why I know it's not a trick of the imagination is that some men want to hear and, of course, they do. But I don't. When a man is put to final rest it should be just that, a rest. Sometimes I feel it's spiritually wrong to bury a person at sea, leaving the body to the mercy of the currents along the ocean floor, twisted this way and that, moving all the time. Perhaps the whispers are a protest they're voicing."

"Excuse me a moment, sir. I think we're swinging."

Glad of the excuse to get away, I stepped over into the wheelhouse. "Tough holding it on the mark?"

The helmsman was the blond-headed kid, Gerlack. He looked at me sheepishly over the binnacle light. "Not too bad, sir. That was my fault. Corking off for the minute."

"I used to play a game when I was behind the wheel, made it up as sort of a contest between me and the mark. Breaks the monotony. You allow yourself one degree each side of the mark and time the number of minutes you can keep it boxed there. When the head falls off you try it again, keep bettering your time."

He looked politely interested. "Sounds like a good idea, sir. What was your longest time?"

"Eighteen minutes, I believe." I heard the tapping of Sloan's cane against the deck, making his way to the ladder. I went out on the wing again.

"If you'll precede me down the ladder, Martin, I'll manage to my cabin alone."

I did that, staying about two steps below him in case he fell. He managed O.K., reaching the bottom puffing from the exertion. I said good night and started back up the ladder.

"By the way, Martin, I see we're running a little shorthanded?"

"We gave all hands a small cut, sir, and a few didn't like it. They left before we sailed."

He gave a little sigh and leaned forward on his cane. "Necessary economy, I suppose. I don't know what's to become of shipping, Martin. Can't recall anything ever like it. I remember in the days of sail a man would never lack for a berth."

"I hope you don't mind too much about that

salary cut. It seemed like a good idea until things pick up."

He shook his head. "Joyce has been harping on that point for months, and I suppose she's right. Perhaps we can make it up to the crew later."

At two o'clock she came up on the bridge and joined me out on the wing. She wore a black woolen dress, belted tightly at the waist, a white silk scarf around her neck. The wind blew her hair back. The sky had cleared and in the pale moonlight she looked younger, fresher, like a coed set for a date.

"Couldn't sleep, Martin, so I thought I'd join you for a little air."

"Is that wise?"

She linked her arm through mine and drew me down so our elbows were on the railing, arm in arm. She rubbed her cheek against mine. "Is what wise, darling?"

"You know. Being up here like this. Suppose he comes up again?"

"He won't."

"What makes you so sure?"

"Stop being a worry-wart, darling. All you have to do is listen for his cane tapping and you know just where he is. Right now he's fast asleep."

"That helmsman behind us isn't."

She craned her head back at the wheelhouse. "He's not far from it. Besides, he can't see us with that light shining in his eyes. Will you stop your worrying? They're quite used to seeing me up here, anyway."

"Suppose Sloan wakens and decides to come up. He wouldn't like it, seeing you here at this hour."

She looked surprised. "Oh, that's right, you wouldn't know. He takes a sedative with his hot milk after the night watch, then sleeps right through until eight, sometimes nine. After midnight the ship could fall apart and he wouldn't hear a thing."

"All the same, you've got to watch your actions on board a ship. Talk, you know. At sea there's not much else men do except gossip."

"They're really worse than women, aren't they?" She nuzzled her cold nose against my cheek. "I suppose I should be a little ashamed of myself the way I acted the other day. I'm not, Martin. Know why? Because I'm in love with you. There, I've said it. Cold sober and—well, just cold."

"It is cold for a July night."

"That wasn't the subject. The lady said she was mad about you. Now you're supposed to say you adore the lady."

"You know I do."

"My God, you lie badly. You should always make it a point to tell the truth—at least, to me."

"O.K., I like you."

"A whole lot?"

"A whole lot."

"Might it be that you love me in a light way?"

"That's it, I guess."

She put her lips close to my ear. "Suppose you tell me all about it over a good-night cigarette. At four in your room?"

"Joyce, that's no good. Not aboard."

"Put your arm around me, Martin. I'm still cold."

"Joyce—"

"One kiss?"

I kissed her, keeping my back to the wheelhouse. When I tried to pull away she pressed in closer, molding herself against me. Her voice was low and urgent.

"Martin, I just can't help this! I can't. I feel like a ninny propositioning a man, but I can't help it."

"Listen, Joyce, this can't work out. Not aboard ship. It's too risky."

"You'll be off at four. No one would be in the

passageway at that time of morning."

"You never can tell."

"I'll be carrying a ledger, just as if I came in to talk over the accounts."

My God. A ledger, at four in the morning.

"Joyce, we'll meet somewhere in Shanghai. That would be the best way, the safest."

She pouted. "Three weeks away? You're not a bit flattering when you say you could stay away from me that long."

"But it's the best thing to do. Believe me."

"All right, darling. In Shanghai."

When Garrett came up I kept him company for a half hour, talking old times over some coffee, then I went below.

"Don't put the light on, darling."

I dropped my hand from the switch. In the dim light coming from the ports I made out the long white stretch of her body lying on the bunk.

I tossed my hat on the bureau and poured myself some brandy. "You're enough to drive a man nuts. What happened to Shanghai?"

"I couldn't sleep, Martin."

"I'm warning you there'll be talk if this keeps up. Give these men a thread to work on and they'll weave a rug before we dock at Shanghai."

"My, I never would have thought you were the cautious type."

"If *he* ever gets wind of it, how long will I last aboard?"

"Stop worrying about Ezra. He hardly knows what day it is sometimes."

"You're underrating him. He may be old and crippled, but he's not dumb."

"I didn't say he was dumb. I said to stop worrying about him."

I took my time lighting a cigarette.

"Will you put that match out! You'll have me

blushing."

I put it out and sat on the edge of the bunk.

"Like it aboard the Trader so far, darling?"

"It's fine, except for Sloan's whispering."

"Oh, that. He gives me goose pimples, too, when he talks about it."

"You have them now. Cold?"

"A little. Gosh, your hands are rough."

"The cross you'll have to bear, I guess."

"But I like them that way. They feel so strong."

"If you like them, that's fine."

"Darling, let's not talk for a while."

We didn't talk for a while.

"How did you ever come to marry Sloan?"

"Such a question to ask! I'm disappointed in you, Martin. You know the reason as well as I do. As well as everybody aboard, for that matter."

"I meant it's odd that you two would ever meet on common ground, where you'd even discuss marriage. He must be nearing eighty."

"Seventy-four."

"Seventy-four, then. I know he can't help the way he looks, but he *is* ugly as they come, and I can't see how he ever got around to asking you, or you accepting."

"We're not really married, Martin."

I twisted my head on the pillow to look at her. Her head rested in the crook of my arm, the dark light from the port tracing her profile.

"Oh, we had the ceremony, all right, but that's as far as it ever went. It was a bargain, really. I had one of those jobs taking photos in the Sambi—that's a cellar club, just off Market. Know the place? Well, Ezra was at a table one night and I asked if he wanted his picture taken. He was sitting in one of the darker booths, so I didn't really get a close look at his face when I asked. If I had, I guess I wouldn't have approached him. I *know* I wouldn't have.

"Anyway, he said yes, and when I brought the pictures to him he asked me to sit with him a while. I don't know why I did, unless it was because he looked so pathetically embarrassed about his appearance. He asked if I ever saw anybody more ugly, as if it were some sort of joke."

"Tough thing to answer."

"Oh, you're not supposed to answer it. He always says that to people he meets, thinks it makes them more comfortable."

"So what happened? He dated you?"

"Not at all. The entire courtship, if you want to call it that, took place right at that table, that same night. He spoke for a while about himself and the Trader, then he started telling me how beautiful I was, how he'd been watching me from the outer bar for— Guess how long, Martin?"

"Can't guess."

"Two years! Imagine it, Martin. For two years, each time the Trader was in, he stood at the outer bar, watching me walk around with the camera, trying to get up the nerve to come in and take a table. He joked about it, I remember, saying his feet were hurting so much that night it gave him the courage to sit at a table where he'd meet me. Then—point-blank—he asked me to marry him."

"Wasted no time."

"Really, that's just the way it happened, that fast. He explained it very carefully, that it would just be a companionship affair and he'd want nothing more than that, sleep separately and so on. Wanted me around him, and with that he'd be satisfied. It was to be a bargain. Stay with him his remaining years and as his widow I would have the vessel. He said he had no one to leave it to, anyway."

"You'll earn it. I don't think I could stand much of that whispering business."

"Oh, he doesn't speak much about that anymore. He knows I don't like it. He's really quite considerate."

"I never said he wasn't. What did you do before the night club stint?"

"This and that. Studied nursing for a while but didn't like the dirty work attached to it. Some modeling then, salesgirl—like you, a number of things. Even worked in a carnival in El Paso for a year. You wouldn't believe what my job was."

"Don't tell me it was watering the elephants."

"Not quite that bad. I was the hoochie-cooch come-on for a side show. You know the kind of act. The pitchman points the cane and the girl grinds and bumps a little and you think for a quarter you get more of the same inside, a lot more. You don't really. You get a bearded lady who is really a man, a very fat man with big—you know what I mean, and other things like that."

"Hoochie-cooch, eh? I'll bet you were good?"

"There were some that thought so."

"You'll have to show me the act some time."

She turned on her side and slid her slim arm across my chest, tucking her head under my chin. "Sorry, darling. I'd need a costume."

"Not for me. I'm pretty broad-minded."

"Somebody's being fresh."

"O.K., I'll settle for a costume. What kind did you wear?"

"Oh, one of those two-piece things with tassels. You know, when you start moving it sways, and then the yokels start reaching for a quarter."

"Where were the tassels located?"

She bit my neck. "You're being fresh again. Get me a cigarette, darling."

"You don't want a cigarette. Listen, it's almost daybreak. I think you'd better go. Crew will be up and around soon."

"No one uses this passageway except you and me, so will you please stop worrying?"

"Well, we could do with some sleep, you know."

She traced the outline of my jaw with her finger. "You're very handsome, Martin."

"I'm beautiful."

"I mean it. Isn't it funny that some men don't know when they're attractive to women?" She raised herself on one elbow, her face over mine, blocking out the gray light from the port. She started rubbing noses. "Love me, darling?"

"Sure."

"I love you very much, you know. Very, *very* much. You don't really believe me, though, do you?" she said, while her eyes scanned mine.

"Sure, I believe you. Why shouldn't I believe you?"

She sank down again, nestling her lips against my neck. "Rub your hand across my shoulder. I want to feel the roughness. Hmmm, nice...." Her fingers went through my hair. "Such a strong man. That's what intrigued me so the first time I saw you, standing at the door in the hotel room. You looked so hard, your face so handsomely brutal, as if it were chiseled from stone. I just couldn't let you get away. Are you glad?"

"Glad of what?" I was having a tough time keeping my eyes open.

"Glad I didn't let you walk out the door?"

"Oh—sure."

"My big gorilla. Kiss me."

"Listen, you'd better go."

"Kiss me first."

The sun was up when she left.

Chapter Five

Skippers working under percentage and putting on the squeeze are never popular. I was no exception. Phelps had arranged a working schedule for deck scaling, and when the deck hands started the job their general beefing and comments about "that money-grubbing Polack bastard" made almost as much noise as their hammers. Ferguson and his gang also went out of their way to show me where they stood. Ferguson gave me the silent treatment and that was O.K. with me, but his men started a routine when they came topside for an occasional blow, spitting in the gutter when I happened to be passing by.

I took it for a few days until I had the feel of the ship, then jammed it into the black gang by giving Ferguson an order to have his men flush the main deck nightly until they broke themselves of the spitting habit. Then I got hold of Phelps and reminded him that part of his job was deck supervision, that I didn't mind being called fancy names but I did mind hearing them. I made it plain he would keep a controlling hand over the men or Garrett would step up as deck boss and he'd step down. He didn't like being told off again and neither did Ferguson; and when Sloan invited all officers to dinner that same night, Joyce tipped me off in advance that they'd been crying on the old man's shoulder. Sloan, it seemed, figured the dinner would be a diplomatic way to get to the bottom of things and see what was going on without poaching on the authority he'd given me.

Garrett was on watch and unable to attend the dinner, but Phelps and Ferguson were there. Joyce acted the hostess, wearing a low-cut gown that had Silva's eyes popping every time he leaned over to serve her.

After the main course Sloan passed cigars around, settled back in his chair, and in a friendly way started to lay the law down to Mr. Phelps and Mr. Ferguson without so much as asking a single question. That neither one expected him to take this tack was evident by their long faces. They couldn't understand this one-sided attitude against the complainants. I could. An hour before the dinner I had taken Sloan to the forepeak and driven a chipping hammer through an eighth-inch-thick plate, a plate I had selected in advance, maybe the rottenest one aboard. When the old man saw the edge of the hammer pierce the metal he was shocked by the neglect and said so. I mentioned casually that there was machinery below in no better condition, and he shook his head sadly. When he went limping back to his cabin it wasn't hard for me to guess that Phelps and Ferguson would do any future crying to slightly deaf ears, and so it didn't surprise me when Sloan started to call the pair down.

He did it gently, though, carefully explaining that the Trader was getting by when other freighters were failing solely because of his long acquaintance with scores of agents on both continents. He spoke at length of the folly of any business depending solely on good will without making some effort to trim sails when the going was rough. Then he concluded with an admonishment.

"In the past, gentlemen, I've made little demands on you, perhaps feeling conditions would improve. I had no wish to disrupt the family atmosphere aboard. It's an atmosphere I find comfortable to live in. But now that temporary measures are being taken as insurance against rougher weather, I must ask each of you to co-operate fully with Captain Lewandowski—particularly where it concerns the upkeep of the ship. Captain Lewandowski is the sole boss aboard this vessel. That must be understood.

Now suppose we all have a drink together and forget this little scolding." He gave Phelps and Ferguson a smile and leaned over to fill their glasses personally. You couldn't help respecting the way he'd handled the matter.

When I left later to relieve Garrett I was feeling pretty good. All along I had been wondering if I might be caught in the middle once Joyce and Sloan clashed on just how far we could go to save money. But it was plain he was coming around to her side, a bit anyway, and it suited me fine. My job would be that much easier. I was satisfied with the whole setup, except for one thing: Joyce every four A.M.

I mean *every*.

She was crazy to believe it could go on any length of time without attracting attention. A ship at sea is a small world, and when the crew tires of discussing the girls they had at the last port they turn to the food and the bridge-house occupants, in that order. With a woman forward they skip the food and let their imaginations run, and when there *is* something going on up there you don't have to hear their buzzings, you can feel it.

Garrett cornered me in the paint locker one morning and reported some of the talk he'd overheard. He told me nothing I hadn't been hearing myself.

"Forget it, Pappy. The crew's looking for something to chew on. They're hot under the collar because I've got their noses to the grindstone, and that's all there is to it."

"Sure that's all, Martin?"

"That's what I said, Pappy! Now let's all mind our own business and get back to work." I was sore, plenty sore. A dozen times I had spoken to her about it and she had shrugged it off; Sloan was asleep, our passageway was private, so why worry?

Garrett put his hand on my shoulder. "Martin,

lad, minding my own business is something I like to do, but I don't want to see the old man hurt."

"Taking plenty for granted, aren't you? Suppose you let me get on with this inventory, and maybe you too have something to do, no?"

He dropped his hand but stood there. "Martin, you can be hurt too. That woman ... well, there's something about her I don't like. Maybe it's the way she looked the night Sandora died; so unfeeling, so cold, her eyes never leaving the body."

"The woman was a nurse, Pappy. They can take it. That explain it?"

He rubbed his chin and shrugged: "All right, Martin. I just hope you'll think of a way to curb the talk aboard before it gets out of hand."

That night I laid it on the line when she came up to the bridge, reminding her Sloan was neither blind nor deaf and would know the score soon, if he didn't know it already. She carried on for a while, then finally agreed to do all our meeting ashore.

Sloan was waiting for me in the flying bridge a few nights later, a place he hardly ever visited because of the climbing. It was raining and he was standing there in the dark, in that oversized blue coat of his, bareheaded, gazing at the sea. It was the tip-off that something was on his mind this night besides his old buddies whispering to him from the deep.

"Pretty damp night, sir."

With the cold rain trickling off his bald head it was a classic understatement. He didn't turn.

I started to leave.

"Martin ..."

"Yes, sir?" The lid was off the kettle, all right. Would he put the question point-blank? I didn't think so. That would amount to an accusation and condemn her also. He had proof of nothing, so it would be a stalemate.

"Martin, I wonder if you know what it means to

be ugly all your life. Really ugly." He spoke slowly, as if he'd thought a lot about it and was choosing his words with care. "So much so, Martin, that you're repulsive even to men hardened to the sea and its rugged ways. And lonely. The two go together, Martin. When you're ugly, you're lonely. But I guess you know that. You're an intelligent man."

He paused and half turned, but didn't look directly at me. "Martin, do you know what you think about when you're lonely?"

He didn't wait for an answer. "You think about a woman, Martin. Not in the usual sense, you understand; that's a cheap thing, for sale anywhere. But when you're really lonely you think of a woman you can sit with and talk the day over, someone who would be concerned with the little things that sometimes worry a man and perhaps mean nothing. You think of someone you can talk to, about the weather, about the new suit you're thinking of buying. Maybe she'll even help you pick it out. That's the kind of woman you think about, Martin."

I had a slicker on, but the rain was finding its way down my neck. A fine time and place he'd picked.

"Of course, Martin, there's a bright side to being lonely, if you can call it a bright side. You can work without interruption, direct all your time to a career. And accumulate money, plenty of it in time. There isn't much else you can do but save your money because there's no one to spend it on. And maybe someday you'll own a vessel like this one.

"But you're not happy, Martin. The ship's an empty thing, a symbol of your frustrations. You go on thinking of this woman, dreaming of her, until you know exactly how she looks, how she dresses, how she speaks. Then—then one day you see her...." His sunken eyes blinked against the rain.

I put the collar of my slicker up. It caught the rain and made it worse.

"It was hard to believe my good fortune when she actually accepted me. Of course, I had no false illusions why she did. It was the security that appealed to her, the vessel she would someday inherit. Still, I was satisfied. She was the woman I had dreamed about, and when she looked at me with neither pity nor revulsion I proposed. It was a grand thing, Martin. After six years it's still a grand thing. I love and respect her, more like a father than a husband, it's true, but that's no matter. That she has returned nothing but the respect satisfies me. I expected nothing more."

He turned slowly, facing me. "There's not much pride in me, Martin, just love. So much love for her there's little room for pride. I'd like an honest answer, Martin: Are you in love with Joyce?"

I frowned a moment over that one. "No, sir. Certainly not. This talk making the rounds—"

He raised a bony hand. "Let's leave it at that, Martin. Just talk." He leaned forward on his cane, the masthead light illuminating his pitted face, the long scar wet and vivid. "Martin, we are both men of intelligence and I'm sure we can agree that an impossible situation has developed, one that could easily become the butt of fo'c'sle jokes. Do you agree?"

"Well, sure, sir. In a way. But this is just something that probably started from a rumor. I think the best thing to do is ignore it and let it die a natural death."

He slowly shook his head. "Martin, the only way to kill this rumor is for you to leave the ship at Shanghai, and I think you realize this as well as I do. I'll give you three months' pay and passage home. In your reference it will state that it was with much regret that I accepted the resignation of an able and efficient man."

Stunned by the abrupt dismissal, I moved out of

his way as he limped over to the ladder on his cane. What could I say? That I didn't give a damn for his woman? That working the Trader meant everything, the woman nothing?

He started to descend the ladder, having a tough time keeping his grip on the slippery rails. Halfway down he stopped and looked up at me, panting from the exertion. "You must learn how to compromise, Martin. Otherwise you will go through life forever hurting people." He paused for breath, still gripping the ladder rails. "Strong men like yourself must always compromise. For if you don't, you see, you will hurt the weaker—as you have hurt me."

After he left I stood on the flying bridge a long while, thinking, but not about Sloan. Hell, if a man couldn't take care of his wife she was bound to go back-fence prowling. I was sorry about only one thing, and that was losing my berth. For the first time I was running a vessel that would pay off nicely once it was in the shape I wanted, and I didn't like the idea of leaving. I didn't like it one damn bit!

The more I thought about it, the madder I got at Joyce for acting as if nobody on the ship could see past the end of his nose.

It was still some time before dawn and I hadn't slept. I was in my room, sitting behind the desk, halfway through a bottle of brandy, when she came in.

She wore a white chenille robe, her hair done up tightly in white cloth curlers. With no make-up on her thin face she had a pinched, washed-out look.

"My God, what a time I've had!" She went over to the bunk and sat down, bowing her head in her hands. "Oh, damn, I forgot I was wearing these." She started removing the curlers. "All night I've been listening to a rehash of the good times we've had together. 'Good times,' he calls it. That's a laugh. I thought I'd go mad before he finally took his milk

Pule in none where
then rule when

and fell asleep."

"Maybe you're satisfied now that the old guy is not as feeble-minded as you thought."

"Martin, I don't blame you for being bitter. I really don't. I guess the passageway gave me a false sense of security. It's been all my fault and I admit it."

That cooled me down some. When she had walked in I'd been tempted to get up and rap her one for being so dumb.

She kept taking curlers out and fussing with her hair. "He gets so stubborn once he's made up his mind I just know he won't change it this time. Martin, whatever are we going to do?"

I tilted the chair back, hooked one leg over the edge of the desk. "I can't answer for you, only for myself. I've got my orders. On the beach in Shanghai."

"I know. He wouldn't come out with the real reason for his decision. He said that the atmosphere you've created aboard was unpleasant and he'd rather you left." She got up and shook her hair out. "Martin, I won't be able to stand it. Going on alone, I mean. Not now. For the first time in my life I have been really happy, for the first time I feel as if I were living."

I lit a cigarette and smoked it and watched her pace the floor, the robe swirling about her long legs.

"Damn him...." She didn't say it loud, just a whisper. But she put everything into it.

She turned, her thin features twisting. "Damn him, anyway! Six years I've given him, six years of denying myself. Six years of my life, and I'm just beginning to live again."

"You didn't expect him to live this long?"

Her green eyes glittered, as if a light had suddenly flamed behind them. "Of course I didn't expect him to live this long! Who would? Just looking at him that night in the Sambi, you'd think he wouldn't last the year. But he did. That year and the next. Six of them! And he looks the same today, as if he'll last another six."

"Or sixteen." I said it casually, without really thinking. There was something about her actions that was puzzling, a false note, as if she were acting out a part, as if she were trying to work herself up to a certain pitch—or work me up.

Her face darkened. "Damn him and his ugly face, his hot milk and his pills! Damn his so precious love! Damn his crooked body! Damn him!" She came over to the desk, clenching her hands, as if fighting to control herself. "I'm not getting any younger, Martin. I don't want to wait six more years. I'm a woman and I want to feel like one. I don't want to go on the way I was before. Not without you, I don't."

I smoked and listened while she went on along the same line and I didn't say anything. Somehow I couldn't shake the feeling that I was watching and listening to a performance strictly for my benefit. She was upset, sure, but why deliberately work herself up into a rage? Why beat her brains out when Sloan held all the cards?

"And what good is it to inherit the ship if I'm too old to enjoy it?" She started pacing the floor again. "This ship is *mine* and I should have the right to live as I please." She stopped and looked at me, her eyes still unnaturally bright.

"Martin, what are we going to do?"

I didn't say anything. What answer was there? Until the old man died he was boss and she'd have to toe the line. Until Sloan died ...

"Martin, there must be *something* we can do."

I looked up at her then. Her eyes held mine a moment, wavered, then lowered. A tingling sensation suddenly shot right down to my toes. My stomach started tightening. It was a crazy thought, but she wasn't talking to hear the sound of her voice. Not this babe.

"Martin, we can't lose each other now."

I studied the end of my cigarette. My stomach kept on tightening. It was crazy; but it figured. It figured down to a T. What else could she be driving at?

"Not now we can't, Martin. Not after having each other."

Like a line from a class-B movie. She was leading up to it, all right. The old man was in the way; without him there would be clear sailing. Martin, dear, just give me the right cue to say it!

I snubbed the cigarette out. O.K., we'd bring it out in the open. "Suppose you say what you're really thinking, Joyce."

She looked at me, frowning. "I don't understand you, Martin."

Just a little country girl waiting to be led along the right path—or, in this case, the wrong one.

"You said before you weren't going to wait six more years. You didn't think of that tonight. A long time ago didn't you tell yourself you weren't going to wait two more? Then you weren't going to wait three more? Like before when you said you weren't going to wait six more?"

The frown deepened between her eyes. "Yes, but I didn't mean—"

"That day you saw me standing in the doorway of your hotel room, Joyce, wasn't it on your mind? The waiting? You were tired of the waiting; you weren't going to wait anymore. When you hired me, wasn't it on your mind that with me or through me you wouldn't have to wait, that something could be done and the waiting ended?"

Her look of shock was pathetic. One stinking actress.

"Martin, do you realize what you're implying?" She gestured vaguely. "I suppose I can't really blame you for thinking—thinking like this. It's probably the way I sound. I'm angry because it's not fair. He said it would be only a few years at the most, and it's a lifetime he's taking from me. It's just not fair." She turned her back, walking slowly across the room. "Martin, I'm so befuddled."

She was befuddled, all right. About as befuddled as a Sand Street chippy on her wedding night.

I leaned back in the chair. "Let's go back to the reason you hired me. You wanted an efficient chief officer, sure, but you must have interviewed a dozen guys that would've done a job. Why me? Could it be you saw a guy that was roughed up more than just a bit, a guy who, if in command of a vessel, wouldn't be so apt to question an old man's passing—not apt, that is, if it meant plenty to him? Could it be you saw a guy who would play along if Ezra Sloan were to join his whispering buddies rather suddenly, and take charge to see no embarrassing questions should arise, or if they did arise that the answers would be waiting? Joyce, that's exactly the way it looks now. Or have I been drinking too much?"

She kept her back turned, facing the blank wall, her shoulders tightening. She didn't say anything. Not one word.

It was a bull's-eye, all right. Or damned close. Maybe only a half-baked plan was in her mind to dispose of Sloan, but it was there, and *had* been there. It had been there and kept alive by the sight of the old man across the breakfast table morning after morning, crippled and ailing but still hanging on. Hanging on for months, then years. Six years of it had given her a bellyful when I came along. When she had hired a mate she'd got one in both senses of the word, and I guess she had been satisfied to let things slide as long as Sloan didn't interfere.

Now that he was stepping into the picture she was all set to start moving—with a little help.

"You're wrong, you know. You shouldn't be

saying such things, Martin." She didn't turn around.

I poured another glass of brandy and drank it slowly. I felt like getting up and slapping her around for even thinking I'd go along with anything like that. But I didn't get up. I sat there wondering how far she'd go, if she actually would put it into words. She hadn't really committed herself. Maybe she wouldn't. Or maybe she was waiting for encouragement.

We'd see. Just for the hell of it, we'd see.

She turned and looked at me, her face tense, her eyes uncertain. Slowly she came over to the desk, pulling nervously on her fingers.

"Martin, really. You shouldn't be thinking I meant such a thing."

"We'll forget what I said, then. As I said, maybe I've been nibbling too much of this stuff."

She nodded, her eyes searching my face. "And we're both tired, and I'm a little more than angry. Otherwise we wouldn't be talking like this, would we?"

"Well, it's not a bad thing to talk out crazy ideas when you think about it a moment. Sort of clears your head, keeps you from doing a dumb thing that looked smart before you put it into words."

"I guess we're all like that. I mean we all get crazy thoughts." She stood there, still pulling at her fingers, as if waiting for me to carry the ball. "I can't help being exasperated at times, the way I'm forced to live. So I suppose like anybody else I get these ... well, crazy thoughts, as you put it."

"What crazy thoughts have you had, Joyce?" I didn't look up at her. I filled the glass again. She moved over to the door and snapped off the lights.

But she didn't leave. She stood by the door in the darkness, her face a pale blur in the dark light of the ports. "Bothered my eyes. Mind?"

"Not at all."

She walked across the room to the port and stood

there gazing out.

"I suppose you know the reason for our layover in Chefoo. Ezra calls it honeymoon time. We stay at a little inn for those two days. Ling's place. It's just off Ta Ping Road, about a half mile below the beach area."

"I know the place."

Her voice dropped a note. "In the evenings we generally take a blanket and sit down by the water. There's seldom anyone around after dark and that's when he goes wading. You see, he's self-conscious about his legs."

"What were you going to do, push his head under and hold it there?"

She wheeled around, sucking in her breath. "Martin, stop talking like that! I wasn't going to do anything of the sort. I just mentioned the place because it's such a lonely spot and—well, you can't help thinking about it; that anything could happen there."

"Sure it could, and that's just the way it would be figured: Anything could happen in a spot like that—including murder. And when a routine investigation started that'd be right in their minds. Before daybreak they'd have you signing your name to a piece of paper explaining just how it happened, right down to the last gurgle."

"Martin, *will* you stop talking like that!"

"That idea was crazy, all right. Ever think of using those pills he takes? Be a natural for the job. An old guy passed away in his sleep."

I think she was sorry she had turned the lights out. She stood by the port, looking across the darkened room at me but not able to see my expression. She'd have liked to, with the conversation going the way it was.

It was a long while before she answered. "I suppose I did. Think about it, I mean. He takes one

Skipper - Boss

pill every night, faithfully. I sometimes thought how easy suicide would be for him."

"Ordinary sedative, those pills?"

"More than that. He's tried sleeping pills and they don't work too well. These have been made up specially for him, and contain morphine sulphate besides a barbiturate."

"Potent stuff, eh?"

"Well, he's been warned against taking more than one a night at his age. Ten is considered fatal, even for a strong, healthy man."

"How do you know?"

She hesitated. "Out of curiosity I spoke to the doctor one time when he was being quite emphatic about the danger of Ezra's using more than one."

"Just out of curiosity, eh? When did you first think of using the pills?"

"I didn't. I—"

"O.K., let's put it this way: How would you get around the autopsy?"

I barely caught the whisper. "There wouldn't have to be an autopsy, Martin."

"You mean over the side? Sea burial? The skipper would have to play along, then. In this case, me."

She didn't say anything. She didn't have to. What was in her mind was perfectly clear. While at sea I was the boss; no police, no coroner. I had the first and last word on any death. With a sea burial all evidence of murder would be gone; not a shred of evidence left to hang anybody on. Once a body went over the side it was a closed case.

That would be the most important point: chuting the body over the side.

"Pretty good setup at sea, Joyce. With the top officer playing along it's perfect." And it was. It was so perfect a chill started playing up my spine.

She moved over to me, a gray shadow in the dark. "Only one thing would stand in the way, Martin:

Ezra has a will. In it is a request to be buried ashore in Sacramento. He has a family plot there. Both Phelps and Ferguson know about the request."

I tried to keep my voice level but something began thickening in my throat at the calm way she could discuss the murder of her husband.

"How would you get around that point? They'd probably object to the sea burial, and say the body should be embalmed at Shanghai and taken to Sacramento."

She put both hands on the desk, leaning toward me, keeping her voice low. I was afraid to look up at her, afraid I'd push her face in.

"I'm his wife. I can say he had changed his mind." She leaned closer, whispering. "Martin, it's easy, all so easy it makes me ill just to think of it. The Trader would be ours. You'll be part owner once we're married. Master and *owner*."

Master and owner. You could taste the flavor of the words. The cherry topping the whipped cream. You could almost commit murder for something like that. Almost.

"So easy, Martin, so easy ..." Even in the dark she must have seen the disgust on my face when I looked up.

"Joyce, it's been quite a talk, educational if nothing else. And I'll slap you silly if I ever hear any of it again. Five days from now I'll be stepping off this ship and what you do then is your business; I'm not setting myself up as anybody's keeper. But until that time, you just keep any crazy thoughts to yourself. I fly off the handle pretty quick, and chances are you'd be missing some of those nice white teeth you have."

She stepped back hurriedly, her expression shaded by the darkness. "Martin—"

"Good night, Joyce."

"Martin, you misunderstood me."

"I understood you perfectly. Good night, Joyce."

She gave me a look I couldn't see and hurried out.

That chill kept playing up my back as I thought about it: A chief officer could murder his captain—or in my case a captain could murder the owner—and get away with it. The important thing was being in sole command of the vessel once the thing was done. If Sloan died tonight I would be sitting as a one-man board of inquiry in the morning, the supreme boss. My verdict would be final. His body could be loaded with poison and the entire ship might figure it that way, but once it slid over the side it was death from natural causes with not a bit of evidence to the contrary.

I fell asleep thinking that it was odd such a thing had never happened—a chief officer poisoning his skipper for the top berth—and thinking how the hell did I know it never happened? Plenty of captains have died at sea and been buried there with the chief officer conducting funeral services. Hell, that was common. How many times had it been murder?

I didn't sleep well that night.

Chapter Six

I was standing out in the darkness of the starboard wing, watching a distant pinpoint of red off the bow. She moved past me over to the railing, the moist wind blowing her dark hair across her pale cheek. It had been almost forty-eight hours since we'd even spoken.

"Angry with me, Martin?"

"No."

"I can see that you are. You've been avoiding even looking at me."

I didn't say anything. I checked the bearing of the vessel ahead again, then I went into the wheelhouse, fooled with the chart, marked it, and smoked a cigarette. Finally I went outside again. She was still on the wing, leaning against the weatherboard, watching the port light on the vessel ahead creep across our bow.

"It always amazes me how you gauge so accurately whether or not there's danger of collision. I think if it were left up to me I'd be shouting for the helmsman to throw his wheel over."

She was trying to clear the air. I went along. "It's not so much a matter of judgment as it is the bearing change. If the bearing changes appreciably, that's it; the other ship's not headed for the same spot you are."

"What happens if you *are* both headed for the same spot, and each ship decides to change course at the same time to avoid a possible collision? Seems to me there'd be a terrible mix-up if each ship turned inward, thinking to pass astern of the other."

"Can't happen. Vessel having the other to starboard must do the changing, the other holds course and speed."

"Oh, I see." She turned, brushing aside her wind-blown hair. "Martin, I couldn't sleep after I left you that night."

"Let's not discuss it."

"But I must. I can't let you go on thinking … thinking—"

"That you'd murder your husband?"

She drew a deep breath. "That's cruel of you. It was all talk that night. Silly talk. Haven't you ever said things you later regretted? Haven't you ever said things when you were carried away by anger?"

"Well, sure."

"And didn't you, yourself, comment on the—the subject, giving your views? My God, Martin, I didn't dream you'd misconstrue my words, their meaning. I just kept talking because you were, because you said it was the best way to get rid of silly ideas. And we all have silly ideas, just as you said. We can't help thinking about how easy this or that would be if a certain thing happened—even when we don't want it to happen. Everybody thinks bad thoughts at times: it's only human to do that."

Her eyes were pleading as she stepped close to me. "Martin, I can't have you thinking these horrible things about me. They're just not true."

She wasn't kidding me. I knew the score. Maybe the idea had now been frightened from her mind, though, so I was willing to forget the whole thing and said so.

She was relieved and showed it.

"Martin, somehow I think we can clear up this whole mess, allow you to continue as the Trader's captain. I feel we might work something out between us."

"It doesn't depend on what *we* do, but on Sloan. He's calling the shots."

"You *do* wish to continue on the Trader, don't you? I mean three months' pay and a passenger liner home doesn't appeal to you more, does it?"

Damn right, it didn't appeal to me more, not at the price of a command. Another command might be a long time coming; another setup like the Eastern Trader might never come.

"I think it would be easy, Martin, to convince Ezra it would be unfair to discharge you in Shanghai. You could say it would jeopardize your chances for other employment to be dismissed this way in the middle of a voyage. Then we'll have a whole month if he lets you stay."

"You figure on making him change his mind during that month?"

She almost bubbled with eagerness. "We might try, Martin. I think secretly he admires your—your forcefulness. Perhaps you could try to get a little friendly with him, talk to him about his sailing days, and about the Trader. Perhaps talk about what he could do to improve things aboard. You know: confide in him about the small daily matters you handle. He'd like that sort of thing. You could even ask him for advice occasionally, make him feel he's still needed, that he isn't entirely helpless. Oh, Martin ..."

She put her hand on my arm. "Martin, it might work. It might. If he gives you another month we'll act cool to each other and try to plant the idea in his mind he was mistaken, that the rumors were actually rumors and nothing more."

I thought it over. It sounded good; it might work, at that. Certainly worth a try. In a short while I was slated to be back on the beach with a million other slobs, all squirming at the bottom of the pile.

It was worth a try, all right.

"Has he said anything to you since the other night, how he feels about the so-called rumors?"

She shook her head. "Not a word. He'd never come out with anything hearsay."

"O.K., I'll drop in on Sloan tomorrow morning. Say, at nine. You be on hand. With you there the subject will be a delicate one and he shouldn't object too strenuously to my staying aboard until we reach Frisco. I'll have a good reason thought up for staying, but you make it a point to be there anyway."

I walked her over to the ladder. She turned suddenly and her arms slipped up around my neck.

Her lips were cold and tasteless.

"You feel differently about me, don't you, Martin?"

"I thought you said we were to act cool toward each other."

"We can *act* that way, but it doesn't mean—"

"Listen, Joyce, let's clear something up. Maybe you like me, maybe a whole lot. But let's stop making like it was the romance of the century. You and I are cut of the same jib in some respects and it suited us to be together. That's as far as it went. And if you're interested in seeing me hold on to this job, you'll stay away from my cabin. We'll not only *act* cool, but live it that way."

She smiled faintly, as if embarrassed. "I suppose you're right about the way we feel, but I think it would have been nicer to call it 'love.'"

"So you see, sir, it's not a simple matter of my stepping off at Shanghai. If you found no fault with my work, then in all fairness you should let me leave so it will appear I'm quitting the ship for another berth. The bad impression I'd create on leaving the Trader in Shanghai and taking other passage home would be difficult to explain away to my next employer."

Sloan pushed aside the magazine he had been reading and drummed on the table with his bony fingers. I had walked in on him alone. Joyce. Where the devil was she?

"I'll make it quite clear in the references I'll be giving you, Martin, that you're an able and efficient man. We have already spoken of that. I think a letter acknowledging your capabilities will be sufficient."

"Perhaps, sir, and then again perhaps not. The men aboard will speculate on my leaving and attach a certain significance to it, regardless of reference. That sort of thing gets around in shipping—" I shut up quickly, sorry I had put it that way.

Sloan didn't look up but his crooked mouth had tightened. Tiny dark veins suddenly stood out in his hollow temples. Before he could speak I gave him the line I'd worked out beforehand.

"Well, I didn't care to bring this up, sir, because it doesn't place me in a very good light. But, as a matter of fact, I had considered my employment aboard the Trader more or less temporary. I mean I had in mind an opening on a tanker now being fitted in Diego. I

was told she was to be ready for the first of
September, just about the time I thought we'd be back
in the States, that it would be mine if I wanted it. I
hate to keep going over this same ground, but the
owner expects me to give him my decision when we
return and I don't think he'd be too happy about my
returning as a passenger on another vessel. I'm sure
you see my point."

He frowned and traced his finger across the
magazine cover. "Shipmasters resign for a number of
reasons."

"Ezra." She came in at that moment from the
inner stateroom. She wore a gingham dress, her hair
parted and braided on each side. "Ezra, I couldn't
help overhearing and I think it's about time we
cleared up a misunderstanding. I've heard about this
loose talk aboard, but never, never did I dream you'd
pay the slightest attention to it. It seems you have. All
right, I'll explain: It so happens I was in Captain
Lewandowski's stateroom about ten days ago, when
perhaps all this talk started; no more than ten
minutes, if I recall correctly. It was late at night, also
true, but I couldn't sleep. The Captain had just come
off watch and we started to discuss the accounts. I
can see now it wasn't the wisest thing to have done,
but it's just one of those things we do and later
regret."

Sloan shifted his weight uncomfortably in the
chair. He didn't say anything. He kept studying the
magazine cover. He figured she was lying but he had
to play it her way. To say what he actually thought
would throw a barrier between them and he didn't
want that. At any price he wanted their way of living
to go on.

She came over and put her arm across his
shoulders, her eyes on me. "You said you had a
tanker waiting for you, Captain?"

"That's right. The Barrier Straits. I was first mate

aboard her two years ago. Jenkins—he's the owner—propositioned me in Diego before we left there."

"And you believe it may affect your getting this position if you leave us before we return to the States?"

"It certainly is a possibility. Particularly when I have only a year under my belt as a master. Jenkins might get the idea I couldn't handle the Trader and was beached at Shanghai. It wouldn't look good, I can tell you that."

She looked down at Sloan and sighed, as if she were extremely exasperated. Her acting was improving. "Ezra, how can you think of letting the Captain leave under a cloud? And what about me? Is my name to be bandied around in the fo'c'sle because of an innocent indiscretion?"

He pushed the magazine aside. His voice was low. "All right, Martin. Your services will be terminated in San Francisco."

She patted his bald head. "Darling, that's the sensible thing to do."

Sloan gave me a side glance as I turned to leave. There was a hidden shrewdness in his old eyes that told me he wasn't fooled by that caress, that he had a pretty good idea it had taken more than an innocent indiscretion to create the talk aboard.

Chapter Seven

Deliberately ingratiating myself with anybody was not to my liking, but the following morning after Sloan O.K.'d my staying aboard I set in motion the little campaign Joyce had spoken about. I walked in on the old man after breakfast with an armful of papers, suggesting we spend a few minutes going over a detailed overhauling analysis I had drawn up, one I had intended to use over the next six months to recondition the vessel at a minimum cost.

He was somewhat hesitant at first, but too much the seaman at heart to let personalities interfere with the welfare of the vessel. He asked me to sit down.

I was damn proud of that analysis. It covered everything from the keel to the wire rigging, and as we got into it I could see Sloan's reserve melting. "And there's this item, sir: the replacement of wire. Now, that's a major expense with any vessel running dry freight. In the past we've been buying new stuff on the West Coast and selling the old for junk. Now that's wrong; at least, for any ship touching Asiatic ports. You can pick up English wire in Shanghai much cheaper. And instead of junking the old stuff you can reel and peddle it to these foreign tramps who'll use it until it falls apart."

He thought about it a moment, and nodded. "True."

On the table were a decanter and glasses. He reached over and pushed the decanter an inch or two my way.

"No, thank you, sir. Bit early for that. Another point, along with overhauling rigging are these blocks. Instead of complete replacements in the States I suggest you drop a hint to the new wire supplier that you're expecting him to overhaul the blocks, billing you only for part replacements."

Item after item I pointed out methods of saving money and gradually bringing longer life to an old freighter. On paper we traveled the length of the ship, from compartment to compartment, from the bilges to the main deck, and after an hour of it you could see the sparkle coming to Sloan's eyes, his enjoyment of something close to his heart: the vessel. You could tell it had cost him a lot to hand over the reins after so many years on the bridge, that he'd be tickled silly to share in the shipmaster's daily problems again.

And I'd see to it he would share them for the next month, at least.

"How did the conference go?"

"Not bad. Friendly, considering everything."

I stood beside Joyce near the well-deck railing, watching a line of seagoing junks drift by. It was a clear day, a stiff breeze from the northwest whipping a dirty froth in the ridges of the yellow troughs. On the last junk to pass, a huge green and orange job having evil-looking silver eyes painted on the bow, an old man began excitedly jumping up and down on the sculling deck, waving his arms to us. When he saw Joyce turn her head his way he stopped jumping and made an obscene gesture. The half-dozen coolies operating the sculling oar turned then, glancing back at us. You could see them grinning, their teeth white against sun-blackened faces.

Joyce looked away. "Martin, why don't you change the watch list, so you're on the eight-to-twelve? Ezra likes to stay up an hour or so in the evenings and talk. Why shouldn't he talk to you?"

"Good idea."

"He can go on for hours about the sailing days, without being too boring about it, either. You might give him a cue."

"You'd make a good general."

She laughed, her cheeks dimpling, her green eyes coming alive. For a moment she was completely relaxed and she looked almost pretty.

"Darling, that's the wrong kind of flattery to use on a woman. Completely wasted. If you said you admired my dress, that would be something accomplished."

She was wearing a tight-fitting blue polka-dot number, a thin satiny type of material that the gusty wind molded against every curve and hollow. It was the type of dress a woman doesn't wear on the open decks of a freighter, not with twenty men around who'd been almost a month at sea. I felt like telling her so but didn't.

"No comment? Well, that's a man for you. And just for that you can buy my dinner as soon as we reach Shanghai."

I looked at her. "Thought the less we saw of each other, the better."

She returned the look. "Anything wrong in having dinner together in a restaurant? Ezra never goes ashore in Shanghai."

"The crew does."

She lifted her eyes in mock surprise. "My, what a scandal that will make! Two people having dinner. Just for being so silly, you can also buy me champagne."

"Can't do a thing with him, Captain. Cutrone was going to throw his hammer at me when I ordered him back down."

"O.K., we'll have a look."

I went down with Phelps into the forepeak. Cutrone had been given the job of scaling and cementing the starboard water tank. He'd started the job, then knocked off.

We'd see about that.

He was sitting beside the open manhole, his arms resting on his knees, his heavy face grimy and beaded with sweat. His eyes were half glazed. He was one sick-looking boy.

"I no work in tank, Cap. No matter what you say."

I looked down into the manhole. A drop light hung in there, its yellow glow all but lost in the thick fog of cement dust suspended in the tank.

"Phelps, come over here!"

He came over, his usual uncertain expression increasing at my tone.

I pointed into the manhole. "Go down and check how much chipping has been done."

He lowered himself partly into the tank, felt for the ladder rungs, then continued down, his shoulders and head disappearing.

His head popped up in ten seconds flat, his mouth open, gasping. "I can't breathe down there!"

"Then just how in hell do you expect anybody else to breathe down there?"

"But you said the tank has to be scaled and cemented."

"Do I have to tell you in exact detail how each job is one, Phelps? Good God, man, don't you know enough to put a blower into a tank when it's being scaled?" I looked at Cutrone. "Where's your tender?"

He looked blank.

I turned to Phelps, who was now climbing out of the tank. "You put no one tending Cutrone?"

He brushed off his uniform and said nothing.

I was ready to blow my top. "Phelps, if Cutrone had been a weaker man he wouldn't be sitting here now. He'd by lying on the floor of that tank, maybe alive, maybe dead, depending on how soon you discovered the body. That's what a tender is for. To keep a check on men working tanks. Now I can put up with stupidity to a certain point, but when I can see myself going before a board of inquiry for causing a seaman's death through neglect, that point is reached. You can keep two stripes but Garrett is stepping up to chief officer. As long as I'm on this vessel your only duties will be bridge watches and care of the charts."

I told Cutrone to knock off for the day and went topside. It had been almost five years since I'd witnessed a man being pulled from a gas tank that had been unattended. The senselessness of the death still stayed with me, and the trial that followed when the crew beefed to the steamboat inspectors that the vessel was running shorthanded. The skipper's ticket had been lifted for negligence, and exactly the same thing could have happened to me if Cutrone had died and the crew decided to make something of it.

"Come in, Martin. Make yourself comfortable." Garrett nodded to the overstuffed chair by his bunk and continued shaving.

I sat down and told him he was stepping up to chief officer, and why.

The razor halted and he turned. "I don't call that a smart move, lad. I appreciate the promotion, but Phelps has been deck boss a good many years. Sloan may not be pleased."

"It's not a question of pleasing. Phelps is not a ship's officer. I want him responsible to another mate, so he'll be double-checked continuously."

Garrett thoughtfully wiped the lather from his face. "I just hope you don't jeopardize your own position by doing this."

That had bothered me some, what Sloan would think. I had the feeling that any action I took, if it was for the welfare of the vessel, would be O.K. with the old man, but I wasn't too sure about this.

When Sloan appeared on the bridge that night I told him what had happened that afternoon and the action I had taken.

"I know he's been with you a long time, sir, but he's a man that really needs supervision. Garrett is just the man for that. You can revoke my order if you wish, but for your protection, the vessel's—even Phelps'—I hope you'll let it ride."

He immediately nodded. "I'll let you in on a little secret, Martin. While it was true I needed a chief officer—or captain—to relieve me of physical duties, I also needed a man to act as buffer between myself and the officers and crew. Why? Well, I suppose I'm known as a soft 'touch.' I can't discharge a man as long as he tries his best to do his job. Bad policy, yes;

but I guess I've met up with too much unhappiness myself to do anything to make others unhappy. Phelps, without question, has selected the wrong vocation. Many years ago I tried to speak to him about a position ashore being more suitable."

He smiled slightly. "I went into his room this particular day and he greeted me by saying I was looking well that morning. There was an expectant look on his face because the second mate's berth was open. I suppose you can guess what happened."

"Phelps became second mate."

He smiled again. "As the saying goes, it's a devil of a way to run a railroad." He turned and limped over to the sideboard, looking at the shimmering ribbon of silver leading to the horizon.

Why I even decided to bring up the subject again I don't know. Perhaps it was his friendly manner.

"Sir, I wonder if we could discuss this ... well, the rumors aboard ship. Mrs. Sloan hit it on the head yesterday morning when she tabbed it an innocent indiscretion. It's pretty uncomfortable having you go on thinking—"

He turned and gave me a level stare. His voice was crisp.

"Martin, a man has two lives: his private life and his business life. I am of the belief that one should never interfere with the other. Call it a code, if you will. I follow it rigidly. While you are in my employ I shall treat you in a friendly manner, as I would any other member of the crew. I shall respect you according to the amount of respect your ability commands—which is a great deal. Sometime in the future, should I meet you on the street, it may probably be I will not even speak to you. I don't know." He paused and his voice softened. "I believe my wife's story because I wish to believe it, not necessarily because it's true. I believe your story also because I wish to believe it. I hope it will never be necessary to bring up this subject again. Now if you'll precede me down the ladder ..."

We sailed up the Hwang Pu at dawn. By noon we had unloaded the Fords and some heavy machinery, and were being buoyed near the Bund with the usual groups of sampans crowding around. Each sampan was equipped with a long bamboo pole, a small net on the end to catch the spoiled stores that were customarily thrown to the river coolies.

From the bridge I watched Silva tossing moldy loaves of bread high in the air and getting a kick out of seeing the coolies battle for each loaf, smashing at each other with their poles, risking their necks for the bread. When Garrett went over and snapped a word to Silva, he quit throwing the loaves in the air and tossed them directly into the baskets instead.

Garrett came up to the bridge, his mouth still grim.

"Pappy, you're too sensitive."

"Maybe so. But I've known times a loaf of bread on the table meant a great deal to me. I don't like that man Silva. Never did."

"He's nutty, but harmless. Every ship has its clown."

Garrett's brow went up. "Clown? I'd say he was more than that. Ever hear some of the stories about him when he worked a Greek tramp?"

I signaled to the seaman at the wheel to secure the engines and knock off. "No time for stories now, Pappy. Got business ashore. If I can I'd like to get out of here by tomorrow on the flood."

I went below, put on white ducks, read a note left on my desk that said: "Savoy at one. Don't forget. J.," and went outside to find Silva leaving the ship in a sampan.

I waited for his sampan to make the Bund, then called another alongside, motioning for the sculling boy to drop me off at the same point Silva was reaching.

The Shanghai chandler that the Trader had been dealing with was a hole in the wall with a sidewalk sign saying: "Sam Lee—All Same Stateside Very Honest Merchandise." I waited outside about twenty minutes, smoking a cigarette and brushing aside offers from Chinese kids to meet "fat sister 'Melican man like."

Silva and a tall scholarly-looking Chinese wearing glasses were shaking hands over a dusty counter when I walked in.

"Complete your ordering, Silva?"

He gave me his usual grin. "Yes, sir, Captain. A month's provisions. And it works out close to fifty cents a man."

"Fine, fine." I picked up the order book from the counter, skimmed through the provision list. It was good fare, nothing fancy, nothing too cheap. It totaled $408.

I looked up at the Chinese and asked, "How much rebate, Sam?"

Sam looked profoundly puzzled, as only a Chinese can look puzzled when it might pay.

"Cumshaw, Sam. You savvy? Rebate! Kickback for Cookie. And I'm in one hell of a hurry!"

Sam turned his bookish eyes on Silva, then gave a helpless shrug. "Al'eady pay, Captain."

Silva shook his head sadly as he dug into his pocket. "You're a hard man, Captain. I didn't think you'd deny me the price of a few drinks."

The "few drinks" amounted to eight British pounds. I tossed it on the counter, told Sam Lee to discount the bill that much, that we'd expect the same in the future, and walked out.

My next stop was a money-changer called Smitty who had a profitable side line of leasing coolie gangs. We'd done business before and he hauled out the bottle from beneath his desk when I walked in. He was short, fat, and pig-eyed. Black hair hung from his nostrils. He doffed the skullcap from his shaven head in a little bow without getting up.

"It is good to see old friends, Captain. Forgive my remaining seated. Rheumatics are still with me and I pray I do not offend you."

His only offense was the oily odor you caught when you got too near him, but I didn't say so. I accepted the dirty tumbler of whisky he offered and took a seat.

"Smitty, I need fifty work boys equipped with chipping hammers, Chefoo and back. Nine days, maybe ten. What's the price?"

"To you, Captain, always reasonable." He thought about it, his forehead creasing in thick folds. "Wages are going up these days."

"I thought they were going down. Well ..." I put the glass on the desk and got up. "The work wasn't too important. It'll wait for another time."

He wagged a fat finger at me. "I was about to say wages are going up, but for the sake of old friendship I will forgo my commission."

"One hundred dollars gold for fifty men, ten days. That's all it's worth to me."

Shock spread across his flabby face.

"Ten days' labor for two dollars a man—"

"—leaves you a dollar a man profit. Look, Smitty, another time I'd enjoy the act, but I've a dinner date. Have fifty men aboard the Trader by five o'clock—and I don't mean fifty grandfathers you can get cheaper. Don't pull that one on me again."

He shrugged his acceptance and reached for the bottle again.

"No, thanks, Smitty. I'll take a rain check."

"Darling, you're being an old fuddy-duddy." Joyce leaned across the table and regarded me. "Is there anything more innocent than dinner at one o'clock in the afternoon? Now tell me, is there?"

I signaled to the waiter for the check. "Seems to me you're forgetting we're supposed to convince Sloan everything is on the up and up between us."

"Does that mean we're to act like strangers ashore?"

"Good idea, isn't it?"

She slowly shook her head. "Definitely not. I think it's a horrible idea. And unnecessary. Ezra comes ashore only in Chefoo, and the seamen aren't in the habit of coming to hotels like this one."

I paid the check, tipped the boy, and got up. Joyce remained seated, toying with her fork. "You've forgotten something, Martin. I said you had to buy me some champagne, remember?"

I sat down again, called the waiter over, and gave him the order.

Joyce took out a compact and started making up her face. "Shall we have it brought up to my room, Martin?" She penciled along the outline of her upper lip and studied the effect in the compact mirror.

"You have a room here?"

"I always take a room ashore after a long trip. A night's sleep in a bed guaranteed to remain stationary is restful."

The waiter came over with a bottle, popped the cork, and filled two glasses. I lit a cigarette and watched a man at the next table manipulating chopsticks in a bowl.

"You didn't answer my question, Martin."

"And what was that?"

"Shall we have the champagne brought to my room?"

"I've got at least a dozen things to do in the next few hours."

She snapped the compact shut and put it away. "Important things?"

"That's right."

She switched the subject. "How are you making out with Ezra?"

"Fair, I think. We're getting along, anyway."

"How are you making out with *me?*" She studied the bubbles in her drink.

"Well, how am I?" The subject hadn't been switched after all.

She put her glass down and gave me a steady look. "Martin, this might be a crude way to put it, but don't you think it's as important to hold my friendship as it is to gain Ezra's?"

I was trying to think up an answer for that when she reached across the table and took my hand. "Don't you see how difficult it will be if we continue to be near each other, yet remain so far apart—even ashore?"

I saw myself caught in a squeeze play and told her so. The slightest hint reaching Sloan that business was going on as usual behind his back would quash forever my chances of a permanent command.

Her hand tightened on mine. "Martin, you stop worrying about that command. Together we can work it out. *Together*, I'm sure of it. But if you're to act distant even when we're ashore ... well, it would be easier for me if you weren't around at all, if someone else were in your place."

I never did like ultimatums. "Meaning you'll get a new playmate."

She withdrew her hand. "I don't like the way you put things, Martin." She picked up her bag and stood up. She looked angry, but she didn't move away.

She fussed with her bag.

"Martin, you really owe me an apology."

"O.K., I'm sorry."

"You don't sound it." She looked as if she wanted to say more but she turned and walked away.

I watched the movement of her hips as she

threaded her way among tables over to the elevator, and I wondered if I'd made a dumb play. Having her on my side might mean the difference in how Sloan would feel about me a month from now. If Joyce lost interest in whether I stayed aboard or not, it could be the difference, all right.

I finished the rest of the champagne, smoked a cigarette, and thought it out. Joyce certainly wasn't hard to take, and the risk ashore shouldn't be too great if we used a little discretion.

I smoked another cigarette, then got up and went out to the lobby to the desk clerk.

"Mrs. Sloan's room."

He looked it up. "C-four, sir."

"Asleep, darling?"

"Not quite."

"You *did* want to come up here, didn't you? I mean, you *really* did?"

"Wouldn't have, if I didn't."

"You forgot to bring something, you know. Champagne."

"Want me to order it?"

"Well, not now. Later, perhaps."

"Later, I'll be back aboard. It's one thing for both of us to be away an afternoon and another thing a night. We've got to be careful."

"You're right, darling. And we will be careful. Will you meet me in Chefoo?"

"Small place. Best not."

"But how about late at night, on the beach, say, in front of Ling's? The second night we're there."

"What are you trying to do, give Sloan a ringside seat?"

"Silly, I don't mean while he's awake. At midnight he'll be taking his pill and milk, and I can slip out without his noticing."

"O.K."

"My, I didn't even have to beg you this time. Don't tell me I'm growing on you?"

"Listen, it's four o'clock. I want to be back aboard by five."

"Does it take an hour from here to the Bund?"

"Just about."

"If I were especially interesting would you mind being a little late?"

"Not when you put it that way."

The coolie gang had been aboard about ten minutes when I arrived. They were milling about the decks, poking their noses into everything, and relieving themselves in the gutters. A stench rose from the warm steel decks.

Phelps was looking on horrified.

Smitty's Number One boy came over, smiling and bowing, scraping his bare feet on the deck. He carried a short bamboo cane, an authority river coolies have a solid respect for.

I jerked my thumb aft. "Get those jokers of yours back on the fantail and keep them there. The first one I see forward I'll pitch over the side. And listen, when you get them back there, have them strip. I'll be back for a look-see."

He shook his head, still smiling. "No take off clothes. No sick. I see. I see."

"I intend to see, too. Get them back there and stripped."

I called Phelps over. "Have a line broken out and get these decks washed down. Hook one up aft for that gang to use while they're aboard."

"How long will that be?"

"Ten days. Don't wrinkle your nose, Phelps, because each one of these babies means a hundred dollars' worth of work before we get back here. Better break out some canvas for them to sleep on, too."

I went to my cabin, put on a uniform, and then

went aft, where the coolies were squatting on the deck, most of them still fully clothed. The ones stripped were all healthy and well-muscled, grinning from ear to ear when they stood up to display themselves.

Smitty's Number One boy was grinning too. "Now you see. No sick, Captain."

"How about the rest?"

"All number one. No sick."

"Happy to hear that. Now tell the others to take those rags off."

He stopped looking so happy. He barked out an order and the bunch lined up and began stripping. It's always a risk carrying coolies aboard for any length of time, but you can minimize that risk with an inspection. Sick or diseased coolies will hire themselves out cheap, and knowing Smitty as well as I did, I guessed he'd try to fatten his profit by using some if he could.

I walked down the line, picking out six with running sores, two with signs of goiter, and two others with a suspicious gray tinge to their skins. Another was missing an ear that looked as if it had rotted off. Each time I pointed out a man we wouldn't take, the Number One boy would scowl and crack the man with the cane, as if the coolie'd committed a crime by being sick.

"Tell Smitty to replace these men by tomorrow morning and stop trying to pawn off cut-rate help on me."

He nodded and bowed. "Will do, Captain. Sick men one big mistake. Velly happy you find."

"I'm glad you're happy. I know Smitty will be happy too. Now let's get down to business. Follow me and I'll show you what I want done in the next ten days."

It took me an hour to square away the work assignments, marking out with chalk exactly what deck work was to be done, the number of men for each job, and so on. One man I gave to Silva to overhaul the kitchen equipment, and five I handed over to Ferguson.

When Joyce came aboard in the morning she was holding her nose and I didn't blame her. The sour smell of unwashed bodies was so thick you could almost taste it. "My God, Martin, must you do this?"

"Won't be so bad once we get off the river, on open water." I nodded to Garrett, who had followed Joyce up the gangway. "We're getting away at noon, Pappy. Take a rough inventory of the brass, will you?"

Garrett knew what I meant and moved off to comply. Joyce looked puzzled.

"Do you expect something to be missing?"

"If the Trader's crew is anything like the Balsco's, I do." I led her aft and showed her the large sampan tied to the after buoy. Its canopy was painted a bright red. On the foredeck three brown-skinned girls were washing, using rags soaked in the yellow river water. On the afterdeck an older woman was nursing a baby, squeezing a long flabby breast against its mouth.

"Sometimes they put a small red ribbon on the top instead of painting the canopy, but it means the same thing: Sailor boys don't have to go ashore, they just slide the hawser at night, plenty beer, plenty girls."

Joyce looked interested. "I've seen this sampan here before but never gave it a thought. My, my. Live and learn."

"I bet you'd have given it a thought if you knew the Trader was footing the bill for the beer and favors. Here's Pappy now. By his looks, plenty is missing."

Garrett came over, shrugging. "Looks like they traded off every fire nozzle, Martin. Ferguson tells me he's missing brass fittings, too, but he doesn't know just how many."

"Take a couple of men, hail a sampan, and see if the stuff's still aboard."

Joyce moved closer to the rail, looking down curiously at the girls who were bathing themselves without regard for modesty. "My Lord, Martin. *Every* fire nozzle? They must have had a wild time down there last night. Surely you don't expect the girls to give any of it back?"

"I don't expect to find any of it aboard. But if it isn't, it's going to be paid for. I'm damn sure of that."

In a few minutes a small sampan appeared under our counter with Garrett and two seamen aboard. Garrett stepped over into the call boat, ducking under the canopy. The girls on the foredeck went right on washing and offered no opposition.

When Garrett appeared again he was holding by the collar a sleepy, grubby-faced oiler by the name of Widemeyer.

"They got rid of the stuff, Martin, but here's something left over from the party."

"Send him to my cabin after breakfast, Pappy. He might want to itemize what's due the ship."

"You got it all wrong, Cap! We didn't use brass. We wouldn't do anything like—"

"Shut up, Widemeyer!" I pushed a sheet of paper and a pencil across the desk. "I want the names of the men and exactly what they used for payment. If I don't get it, or you short-change me—and I've got a pretty good idea what's missing—I'm entering a bill against your salary for three hundred dollars."

His jaw went slack. "Geeze, Cap, the stuff don't cost that much—"

"Maybe not, but I want to be sure the ship doesn't get the short end of this. Three hundred dollars charged against you, or a proper account—and who to bill. It's up to you and your pals."

Within an hour Widemeyer returned with a list of eight names and some fifty dollars' worth of brass equipment they'd bartered with. I called it a hundred even to be on the safe side and handed the names over to Joyce for a payroll assessment.

She gave me an amused look. "Only one thing disturbs me, Martin. Just how do you know the ins and outs of this sort of thing so thoroughly?"

"Comes under 'Miscellaneous' in 'Blair's Seamanship.'"

She didn't know whether to believe me or not.

Chapter Eight

On the way north to Chefoo the coolies' constant pounding with chipping hammers, plus our own hands working air scaling hammers, made living aboard pretty miserable. The rank smell that clung to the ship on the humid windless days didn't help matters, either. But it was worth it. The net results would pay off in cold hard cash. For slops and a hundred gold, the savings were running into the thousands.

You could see Sloan was impressed each time he hobbled along the deck to survey the half-naked coolies sweating over their hammers. The completed work for the day was the equivalent of what a large shipyard gang would do at a fancy price, and Sloan's practiced eye saw this immediately.

I made sure he saw other things, too. The first morning, although he half protested that it wore him down too much, I took him below to the engine room. Ferguson nearly had a fit, as I knew he would, because the place looked more of a mess than it really was. A large generator had been taken apart for cleaning and the parts were lying about. The coolies working in the engine room had half the floor plates lifted and were up to their elbows in grease and filth. The general effect was that neglect had been the rule, and now, only now—with Captain Lewandowski in charge—were long awaited repairs being made and general cleaning tended to.

I followed this through each morning, getting Sloan to accompany me on short inspection trips, and I played it cute: If Sloan was due to accompany me to the fo'c'sle, I made sure men were assigned to continue cementing the forward tanks, that there was plenty of activity for him to see. If we made an inspection aft, I saw to it that Peterson, a lanky blue-jawed carpenter, was at work on the fantail railing. Each time Sloan agreed to accompany me on an inspection tour, he ran into the same hustle and bustle.

When Joyce told me the old man was actually praising my work, I didn't slow down but went into straight apple-polishing. On the first evening watch, when Sloan came topside for an hour or two, I went right along with Joyce's suggestion to get the old man talking of his sailing-ship days, a subject he loved. It proved to be a cinch to get him going and another thing to stop him. He went back sixty years to his cabin-boy days, and as he talked on you could almost see the glow on his old face as he described the first clipper he sailed and his struggle for recognition to a third mate's berth. As I listened to him, though, I found myself seeing Sloan in a different light. Instead of an ugly old man I was seeing a crippled and disfigured kid who fought for each berth against the ship owner's prejudice against handicapped seamen. You could almost feel the lonely nights he'd watched city lights from his bridge, yearning to go ashore but knowing he was unwanted socially; and you couldn't help wondering how he ever held on to his sense of humor, not becoming warped in bitterness.

The longer I was in his company, the more I got to

like him, and I found myself wishing Joyce didn't
exist so we could get along better.

Early Monday morning we anchored in Chefoo's
outer harbor, just off the breakwater. After Sloan and
Joyce left the ship, on their way to spend their
so-called honeymoon at Ling's, I went back to the
fantail where Phelps was shooing sampans away. The
sampans were trying to secure their lines, as usual, to
anything they could reach, including our rudder post.

"Don't chase them, Phelps. Let them tie up and
then toss hammers into every boat having an
able-bodied man. Workee, eatee, no cash. Make that
clear. Put a starboard list on her and get them busy on
the port side. And listen: Notify all hands to get their
drinking done today, one day ashore. That applies to
everyone, including officers."

Phelps turned from the rail frowning. "I thought
we were laying over two days."

"We are, but it's twenty-four hours for the crew,
Phelps, and no more. I want to get the most out of
these coolies before we pay them off in Shanghai, and
the only way to do it is to keep the crew working with
them. If anybody's still ashore after noon tomorrow
I'm taking it he's jumped ship and he'll be written
off."

Chefoo was a small place, small enough for
someone to bump into me in the vicinity of Ling's
that second night when I was to meet Joyce. All hands
knew she and the old man were putting up there, and
all they'd have to do would be to spot me there late at
night and a fresh set of rumors would be making the
rounds. Chefoo would be the one port Joyce and I
could hardly escape notice for any length of time.

Up on the bridge I put the glasses on the eastern
part the harbor, where low-lying hills encircled a
horseshoe curve of brown sandy beach. The beach
was studded with bungalows, but near the extreme
seaward point of the curve a line of huge boulders

formed a sand break, and beyond this the beach became a deserted stretch of wild brush and wind-swept sand dunes. Here, set well back from the shore in a grove of trees, the red-tiled roof of Ling's glittered in the morning sunlight.

With the brush and high dunes denying anyone at the inn a clear view of the shore, I found myself feeling easier about the midnight date. I didn't like this hide-and-seek business, but I'd pretty much made up my mind to go along with Joyce, for a time, anyway. Until Sloan O.K.'d my position aboard she could louse things up with one word. And I didn't doubt for one minute that she would if things didn't suit her.

I knew exactly where I stood.

"More trouble than it's worth, Martin."

I stood beside Garrett on the gangway head watching the dozen or so coolies working on the side from their sampans. Garrett was right when he said they would hardly accomplish much in two days, but that didn't bother me. All I wanted was a bright patch of red lead over clean metal to strike Sloan's eyes when he came up this gangway. It would be one more job under way, one more item to tip the scales my way by the time we returned to the States. I wanted those scales so unbalanced in my favor that the refusal would stick in Sloan's throat once I hinted the Trader was more to my liking than the Barrier Straits.

"By the way, Pappy, that order to stay aboard the second night doesn't apply to you. Thought I'd let you know in case you felt like getting slopped up and staying over."

Garrett smiled, knowing I was joking about the drinking part. He seldom exceeded a beer or two, limiting his shore leaves to long walks, picking up a few cheap souvenirs for his wife and kids. At Shanghai he'd gone ashore only to send a money order home, his full month's salary.

"I'll stay aboard, Martin, so the others won't talk about favoritism."

"Look, Pappy, I'm loaded. Take a few bucks and buy a dinner for yourself. Pay it back any time."

He shook his head. "Thanks, lad, but a few dollars means so much at home right now I'd rather keep the sails trimmed."

"Incidentally, did Joy—Mrs. Sloan tell you the chief officer rates a quarterly cut? One per cent, I think. Not much, I know, but it'll mean a little kitty every few months."

He looked surprised and pleased. "I didn't know about that."

I didn't know about it either until that moment, and could hardly believe I'd said it. Lewandowski cutting his own percentage?

I walked away wondering if Sloan's generous ways were getting contagious.

Tuesday at noon all hands had shown up with the exception of one oiler. By nightfall he was still missing, and I went ashore earlier than I had planned, making the rounds of the water-front dives.

I found him in a smoke-filled cellar off Da-Chong Alley, sitting at a small table, joining in with a boisterous seamen crowd, shouting encouragement to a Korean girl giving a performance in the center of the floor. The girl was dressed in a pair of green silk stockings. Her dark supple body looked oily as it writhed under a cone of yellow light.

"Weren't you ordered to be aboard by noon at the latest?"

He looked up at me bleary-eyed, his heavy-muscled face flushed and perspiring. He grinned. "Hey, whataya know, the skipper! Sit down, Cap, an' watch this babe. She's just getting started."

"You've got thirty minutes to get to the ship. Get

there a minute late and you're signed off."

I waited outside in the shadows of the alley. In a few minutes he came out, muttering and swearing. He got his bearings, then lurched over to a ricksha waiting at the curb. When the ricksha disappeared up the alley I went across the way to a small bar and ordered a drink.

The place was deserted except for a drunk sleeping it off at a rear table and a fattish baby-faced blonde at a side booth. Through the bar mirror I watched her powder her nose and tried to finish my drink before she made the approach. No luck.

"Buy me a drink, sailor?"

I motioned to the Chinese barkeep to double the order.

"Thanks a million, sailor. You're a sport. Ain't many around today, I must say." She slid a fleshy arm through mine. She had a damp hairy smell. "I could tell you was lonesome the minute I saw you, an' a sport? Listen, a sport I can spot a mile off."

"What do you charge a throw?"

She tried to look coy. "Gee, the way you put it. Like I was a common—"

"How much?"

She fussed with her hair. "Well, it ain't the yellow stuff, sailor, so it don't come cheap. But you'll have a time."

I threw a five on the bar in front of her. "Take it and get out. I want to finish a couple of drinks alone."

"Well! I never—"

I reached for the five but she beat me to it and stuffed it down her blouse. "I ain't the one to look for charity, sailor. I'm on the top floor."

"Beat it. I said I wanted to drink alone."

The barkeep pushed his thin yellow face over the bar and shook a long finger at her. "Cappee say go 'way! You go. Make chop-chop!"

She glared at him. "You know what I think of you?" She told him what she thought of him in shrill tones and waddled out.

I had another drink, killing time, and at one o'clock took a ricksha along the beach drive. About a quarter mile from Ling's I got out to walk the rest of the way, along the water's edge. Here and there, lying in the sand, were couples, mostly Navy men and Chinese girls. Some of them didn't give a damn or thought it was darker than it was. Near the sand break the shore became deserted.

"Hello, darling."

I slid down a sand dune, trying to locate the sound of her voice in the darkness. Then I saw the cluster of boulders, the pale silhouette of her slim body against the facing of a rock. She didn't have a stitch on.

"I thought I'd take a swim while I was waiting."

"I like your bathing suit."

"Thank you, sweet. The water's refreshing. Join me?"

"I'll just sit here and smoke. You go ahead."

"Now don't be an old kill-joy, dear." She moved away from the rocks, toward the surf. "There's a blanket back there you can put your things on. I'll give you just five minutes before I come out and throw wet sand all over that nice clean uniform."

She was floating some fifty yards out when I joined her. For a half hour we swam around, then she got up the idea of a catch-and-kiss game. She wasn't too strong a swimmer but managed to wriggle and slide out of my grasp each time, laughing and plunging away.

In five minutes I was out of breath, but not from the exertion. Her teeth flashed white over the surface of the water. "C'mon, little boy! I'll give you one more chance." She started to swim in, throwing me fleeting glances over her shoulder.

I caught up with her some twenty feet from the

shore. She didn't attempt to break away this time but pressed against me. At that same moment a rushing comber broke and tumbled both of us head over heels up on the beach.

I landed on my back in the coarse sand, the wind knocked out of me. She flopped over me and grabbed my hair with her hands. She was like something insane that had come out of the sea, her wet dark hair hanging straight down, her green eyes glittering, her teeth bared, making small animal sounds.

"Hey, my back hurts. I'm lying on some pebbles."

She lifted her lips from my neck and laughed softly. "Now you have an idea of what the female species puts up with."

"Listen, let's get dressed. Suppose somebody sees us from the brush?"

"Maybe they'd learn something."

"Maybe. Now if you don't mind moving ..."

We stretched out on the blanket she had brought along. Her head rested on my shoulder. The moon had broken through the clouds and looked like a slice of cantaloupe suspended above us. The night was silent except for the soft rushing sounds of the breakers.

"Martin, it's so wonderful being here like this. As if we were the only two people in the world. Or am I being corny?"

"You are."

"I think it's nice to be corny sometimes. Nice to stop thinking about being smart. What do you want out of life, Martin? Ever think about it?"

"Enough money so I wouldn't have to think about it, I guess."

"Oh, you don't want that. I mean, you do but you want what it will give you. What do you *really* want?"

"Maybe to walk the bridge of a ship that's mine. I

guess every skipper more or less wants that."

She snuggled closer. "When I was a little girl I guess you'd say I lived on the other side of the tracks. On one side of our town was a hill with all the nice homes, on the other side the tenant farmers in their rickety shacks. You know what I wanted most then? To live up on that hill. It was the one thing I constantly thought about. That someday I'd live up on that hill and look down on the town and the other people. I'm being corny again, I guess, but I wanted it then and I want it now."

"Sums it up for everybody, I suppose: looking down from a hill. Only thing is there's damn little space on a hilltop. Plenty room below in the valley where it's darker, though."

"Darling, you surprise me. You sound almost like a philosopher. You came from a mining town, didn't you? What was it like?"

"Well, we had that hill you spoke about, and the valley too. But this valley consisted of long dark tunnels you spent half your life in. You lived in black dust, breathed it, ate it, and cursed it. We buried my mother when she was forty-five. That's a ripe old age after you have six kids and try to raise them on a miner's pay. My old man we didn't have to bury. The company figured it was cheaper to leave him there and throw the kids a few bucks."

"Made you bitter, didn't it, Martin?"

I handed her a cigarette. "No, I'm not bitter. This world is composed of a certain percentage of bastards and always will be. Nothing will ever change that. You can yap about it and scream your head off. You can even go out to break one particular bastard in two. But if you do that you're silly. There's another born that very second to take his place. The trick is to be just a little bit of a bastard yourself so you won't get hurt too much."

"I think I feel the same way, Martin. At home I

was forever getting in trouble for doing things that I knew others wanted to do but were afraid to do. I bobbed my hair when you were practically a tainted woman if you did, and I painted my fingernails one Sunday going to church when the minister had lectured the week before against the use of cosmetics by schoolgirls."

"Regular devil."

She turned on her side and pressed her lips against my ear. "Just like you, darling. Only you hold back. I can't. Hold back, I mean. I want to do everything before I die. I want to see everything and feel everything. I want to take off my clothes and roll naked in the mud to find out what it's like. Crazy, isn't it?"

"Sure is."

She kissed my ear and got up. "Turn your head, darling. I want to dress. I never like to put my clothes on with anybody watching."

I thought this was crazy, too, but I turned.

"Martin, let's go night-clubbing. Keep your head turned. Let's go to some of those places you sailors always go."

"Don't you think you'd better be getting back to Ling's?"

"But I've never been to a night club in China, Martin. I want to go. Tonight. How about that place called Creek Head Inn I've heard so much about?"

I looked around to see if she was kidding. She covered herself with the dress.

"Martin Lewandowski, I said no peeping."

"Listen, you don't want to go to that joint. There isn't a lower dive in these parts."

"Oh, we can at least—turn your head like a good boy—we can at least drop in for a drink."

"Look, Joyce, I've been there. It's no place for a woman."

"Martin, dear, *please*. Don't give me that old story

it's no place for a woman. If it was left up to you men, we'd never do much else but stay at home and have babies. You can look now and zip me."

Creek Head Inn was an ancient clapboard house, located on the remote and lonely outskirts of town. Separated from the road by a narrow creek, it had been built up against a bluff, with a long flight of steps serving as both bridge and stairway leading down to the road. In the darkness the house had the appearance of something bulging out of the bluff, ready to topple if the stairs were removed.

Joyce stepped out of the ricksha, looking curiously about at the gloomy surroundings. She didn't appear nervous.

"Is it closed, Martin? There's no light showing."

"Windows are painted black. These boys like privacy." I tore a bill in two and handed one half to the ricksha coolie. When you visit Creek Head Inn it's smart to have a ricksha waiting in case of a hurried exit.

"Let's go, and don't forget you asked for it."

There's nothing like a merchant-marine uniform for gaining admittance to places where anything goes for a buck. At the head of the stairs a fat yellow face gave me a gold-toothed grin and opened the door wide. He stopped grinning when he saw Joyce.

"No lady, Captain! No likee. Boss man no likee."

"Nonsense!" Joyce moved right past him before he could shut the door. The man looked at me, then shrugged.

We followed him down a grimy hall where a single lantern from the ceiling gave a malaria-yellow tone to the faded walls. At the end of the hall he pushed open a door and stood aside.

It was a small low-ceilinged room with maybe a dozen tables crowding a tiny dance floor. A beat-up piano in the center of the floor was being pounded by an unshaven white man chewing on a black cigar. In the back of the room was a two-by-four bar, and off to the side heavy faded draperies hung from ceiling to floor.

Over the entire room a haze of blue smoke hovered near the ceiling.

We got plenty of cold stares from hard-faced characters sitting at the tables as Gold Tooth led the way to ours. When Joyce was seated she wondered about this.

"They figure a woman will cramp things a bit."

"I'm sure they needn't worry about me."

I ordered beer, bottled and capped.

"Martin, I don't want beer. I'd rather have something stronger."

"In here you're liable to get something a lot stronger than you bargained for if you look a bit prosperous. We'll order beer and open it ourselves. It's safer."

Gold-Tooth left with the order. The guy finished his piece at the piano and one or two gave him a light hand. He flicked the ash off his cigar, gave Joyce a stony look, then got up and went over to the bar to join Gold Tooth. They held a conference, with the Chinese helplessly throwing up his hands. The guy, who was apparently the boss, looked over at Joyce again, shrugged, and meandered back to the piano.

A Japanese houseboy in white shorts carrying a pipe rack crossed the floor. He disappeared through the drapes in the back.

"What's going on back there, Martin?"

"Smoke parties. Dollar a pipe."

The piano player started a blues number. Gold Tooth came over with two bottles of beer, glasses, and an opener.

Joyce gave me a bored look. "Martin, I thought this was such a dreadful place. It's really nothing except for the opium smokers, and you can't even see them. Isn't there a floor show or something?"

Gold Tooth paused in the middle of opening a bottle. "Lady want show? Girl show?"

"Well, why not?"

"Joyce, never mind that. We'll have the beer and beat it. Their shows are not for women."

"Nothing ever is. Stop being stuffy, Martin. I'm not leaving when I just got here. And if there's a show, I want to see it."

Gold Tooth gave Joyce a smirk, filled the glasses, then went over to the piano player to whisper something. The player removed the cigar from his mouth and swung his eyes to Joyce in surprise. He struck a chord on the piano, still looking at Joyce.

The overhead lights flickered and went out.

For a full minute we sat in the dark, waiting, the room quiet except for the scrape of a chair, a cough. You could feel the anticipation building up around the room. Joyce reached over and gripped my arm.

Suddenly a shaft of purple light cut through the darkness from behind us, throwing a spotlight on the floor, revealing a tall, lithe Malayan girl standing motionless, naked, her arms overhead, her palms pressed together, her slanted eyes downcast. For several moments she stood there, her young rounded breasts high, her lean abdomen stretched taut, so motionless that she created the illusion of a black ebony statue.

A soft melody on the piano broke the illusion. The girl's dark eyes lifted and a wanton smile touched her full mouth. Her hips described a slow undulating motion, deliberate and graceful. The tempo of the piano increased slightly. So did her movements.

A silver coin spun into the spotlight and dropped near the girl. She smiled her encouragement, linked her hands behind her neck, and went into a slow-motion squirm, her breasts swaying. Another coin flashed into the spotlight and dropped at her feet. She smiled again and responded with a series of violent movements that were anything but graceful. A shower of coins spilled out onto the floor.

After that it wasn't even a dance.

I looked at Joyce to see how she was taking it. She was leaning forward, elbows on the table, her chin cupped in her hands. She looked amused.

"Ready, Joyce?"

"To go, you mean? Oh, Martin, stop being such a damn puritan."

"What you're looking at is tame stuff for these characters. Things are bound to get rougher."

"Why don't you order another beer for yourself?"

I gave it up as a bad job, got up, and circled the room, moving over to the bar. The houseboy brought out a bottle of beer and poured it. I finished half of it watching the dancer keeping time with a jungle beat, then I went out to the men's room.

Even before I got back I could sense the change of atmosphere. The piano had stopped and the spotlight holding the floor had paled until the dancing girl was just a suggestion of a shadow. But now there were two shadows on the floor, and it wasn't before I reached the table that I made out the giant black, the gleam of his teeth, the whites of his eyes following the enticing movements before him.

The party was getting rough, all right.

I didn't bother sitting down. "Joyce, listen ..."

But she wasn't listening. She was looking at the preliminaries on the floor, her eyes narrowed, her lips parted, her breathing quickened with anticipation.

At the next table I saw two jokers in wrinkled whites go into a huddle, their eyes on Joyce. One grinned and got up. He slouched over, leering at Joyce. He was a good six inches taller than I, bull-necked, and with arms that swung like a gorilla's. He was drunk.

Being drunk would make the difference.

"'S' matter, Cap? No like the show? Why don'tcha go home, then?" He kept leering down at Joyce, moving closer to me as if to shoulder me out of the way. "We'll take care of the little lady."

My knee came up and connected exactly where I wanted it to connect. The leer froze on his face and he went down, slowly and quietly. From the way my kneecap felt, he'd be lucky if he was back in business within six months.

His partner gave me a sickish smile and dropped back into his seat.

"Joyce, make up your mind: Do I carry you out or do you walk?"

She picked up her handbag and got up without a word. She had to step over the guy on the floor.

On the way back to Ling's she had nothing to say, breaking the silence only when we neared the inn and I ordered the ricksha coolie to pull up.

"You didn't have to do that, Martin. Hurt that man."

"I didn't? Listen, you know what those guys had on their minds? It wasn't tiddly-winks with you, I can tell you that. All I had to do was start gabbing with that monkey back there and his partner would've come up behind and parted my skull with a bottle. You think anybody back there would raise an eyelid if they shoved me under a table and took over? Not those babies; not on your life! That'd be just part of the floor show."

"But you started all the fuss. If you had stayed seated and stopped acting the prude, it wouldn't have happened."

"Prude?" I shut up fast. I felt like hauling off and clouting her. There are some things a woman isn't supposed to look at—at least, not enjoy the way she had been doing.

She got out of the ricksha, smoothed her dress, and looked up. "Aren't you going to walk me the rest of the way?"

"No need. You're safe in these parts."

"Kiss me good night so we won't part mad."

She stood on tiptoe, closing her eyes, tilting her face up. I intended only to brush her lips, but she grabbed my head and held the kiss, her mouth hot and working on mine.

When she let go she turned and walked rapidly in the direction of the inn. I watched her until she disappeared in the darkness, then leaned over the side of the ricksha to spit the sour taste from my mouth.

I couldn't help it. Maybe it was Creek's Head Inn. Maybe it was the expression on Joyce's face when the black had joined the performance. Maybe it was the smell of her when she kissed me.

Whatever it was, the sour taste remained in my mouth all the way back to the ship.

Chapter Nine

"Mind if I come in for a moment, Martin?"

"Not at all, sir. Glad to have you." I got up from the desk and turned the leather chair around for Sloan. He came limping in, looking tired.

"I came to ask a favor of you, Martin. But perhaps a little talk first might clarify things." He sat down, placing the cane across his knees.

I sat on the edge of the desk, facing him. I had a pretty good idea of what was coming. We hadn't been ten hours out of Chefoo before Joyce had told me she intended to talk to Sloan about my position. I advised against it but she thought it would be best to get the thought across early that I'd prefer the Trader to the tanker I was supposed to have waiting.

Maybe she was right.

"The only thing I have is brandy, sir. If you'd care for that?"

He waved it aside. "Don't care, for the taste of it."

"That's right, I'd forgotten. Sorry I have nothing else."

"Perfectly all right." He studied his cane a moment.

"It's really difficult saying what I have to say. First, let me say I consider you an excellent skipper. A little rough with the men at times, perhaps more than necessary, but in the main an excellent skipper. I know it is your desire to remain aboard the Trader. Is that correct?"

"Well, sir, I do like in working with you, and I've always preferred dry freight."

"Martin, let's start off by being frank. It is my guess you've never had a tanker waiting."

What could I say? I busied myself lighting a cigarette.

"It's also my guess your hope was to make yourself indispensable, so would consider permanent employment." His crooked mouth moved into a smile. "My boy, don't feel ashamed of your subterfuge. I don't blame you for it. With a berth at stake I don't blame you at all."

"Tough thing, the beach."

He nodded agreement. "Aye, tough it is. To a seaman it can be a prison." He hesitated. "Joyce and I had a long discussion this morning. The main of it was, an injustice is being done you." He went back to studying the cane.

I smoked and said nothing.

"Martin, am I really doing you an injustice?" He raised his head.

I looked him straight in the eye. "Yes, sir, you are."

He sighed and shook his head. "I'll try to rectify that, then. Make up to you in some way for the loss of this position. You see, Martin, I'm not going to change my mind on replacing you. I'll tell you why and I hope you understand."

Right then I came close to hating him. For a minute I had believed he had come in to smooth things over, tell me the Trader was mine. I had even been forming thank-yous in my mind when he pulled the plug out.

"I'm an old man, Martin, and an old man's mind is a funny thing. It lives in the past and the present. Never the future. I can't wait, as you can, for better times, for happier moments. I must have them now. What I'm trying to say is I would feel uncomfortable with you aboard. Perhaps it would wear off in time, but I have no guarantee there is much time for me. I can see myself living a year or two more, and during that time, if I must live among loose rumors, my short time would not be a happy one. I would be constantly faced with a truth I try not to think about, that I am unwanted and Joyce waits only for the day she may be free to do as she pleases. It's been like that from the first, I well know, but before you come aboard there seemed to be no one she had an attachment for, and she was therefore content with our arrangement."

He used the cane to get up, then stood there a moment. "Martin, give me my peace of mind, my year or two of comfort. It's in your power to do that. Joyce is so broken up about my refusal to keep you on that she refuses to speak to me. Now if you, of your own free will, claimed you'd rather not stay aboard, it would ease things. Will you do that for me?"

I no longer hated him. The feeling had gone as quickly as it had come. I was thinking of the chair that had come flying across the room in a Singapore bar, the knife slash, and then the pox when he rounded the Horn. I was thinking I was pretty well off, everything considered, that things could be a damn sight worse.

"Will you do that, Martin? Joyce does not know I'm in here speaking to you. In the month under way, before we reach the States, will you get across the idea you have changed your mind about staying aboard?"

I nodded and snubbed the butt out. As long as I had to leave, I could do it gracefully.

"All right, sir. It's going to take a pretty straight face to say I want to leave the Trader, but I'll try it."

He came over and put a thin hand on my arm.

"Listen, Martin. I didn't come in here asking a favor without having one ready in return. I have many friends in shipping, and as soon as we reach the Coast we'll go to work on your future. It may be only a mate's berth, but we'll see to it the line is a busy one with an excellent chance of command in a short time. How does that appeal to you?"

It didn't. Stepping down never does. You can't go off a diet of cake to plain bread and not taste the difference. But I thanked him and let it go at that.

At midnight the sea began kicking up. Combers broke over the bows, the wind sweeping the spray over the bridge house. Phelps entered the wheelhouse, wiping his glasses and looking concerned.

"Garrett says we're in for some fun before long. Perhaps I should have some deck lines rigged."

"Plenty of time for that. It's circling about two hundred miles out. We're not even on the fringe."

"Maybe we'll run into it after leaving Shanghai."

"Maybe."

I cut more weather talk short and went out on the wing. For maybe ten minutes I stood there watching the bow dip into the dark troughs, the spray rising upward like a silver cloud in the night. I was plenty depressed now that my leaving the Trader was settled. I'd come to really love the old ship. Maybe I'd been over it so thoroughly I knew it too well, what it was and how it would be when it was put into shape. A skipper becomes attached to a ship when he knows it well. It becomes something almost human to him, with its engines and feed lines much the same as a heart and blood vessels. He can feel its aches and pains, and after he mothers it a while it's something that needs him, something that depends on just him and no one else. When he leaves a ship behind, a part of him stays with it and keeps fretting if this or that is being handled properly, or perhaps being neglected. And this was exactly the way I would feel about the Eastern Trader when I left.

When I went below I was in a lousy mood, and it didn't improve when I saw Joyce lying in my bunk. She wore pajamas. Her robe was across the foot of the bunk. She turned her head and her green eyes stared over at me, unnaturally bright in the semidark, as if a green flame were playing behind them. I didn't put the light on.

"You're out of bounds, Joyce. Grab your robe and beat it."

She kept staring at me, not moving. Her breasts rose and fell with quick breathing. Her voice had a husky, breathless quality that was new to me.

"Martin. Come to me."

I took my coat off, wondering what the devil had stirred her like this. "Up and out, Joyce. We've talked about this business before."

Still she didn't get up. Slowly she rolled over, burying her face in the pillow. Her fingers dug into the pillow as she seemed to strain against the bunk.

I poured myself a stiff drink, wondering again what had got into her. It didn't take much to get her started, but I'd never seen her in quite such bad shape.

"Martin, come here."

Well, why not? What did I have to lose? Maybe it would snap me out of it.

I put the glass down without touching it, looked over at her. She was still gripping the pillow, her body taut, perceptibly moving. She wanted to roll in the mud, did she?

O.K. We'd give the devil a show.

"Martin."

"Yeah?"

"I didn't tell you when I came in."

"Tell me what?"

"I was so upset I thought I'd break down if I started to talk about it."

"You're talking in circles."

"Please don't be angry that I didn't say something right away."

"Say what? For God's sake, Joyce—"

"He's dead, Martin."

Chapter Ten

"Just like that, eh? Passed away in his sleep. You didn't call anyone, just locked the door and came to my room."

She nodded quickly, drawing the robe around her. She went over to the desk and got a cigarette there, eying me nervously while lighting it.

I got up from the bunk. A spring inside me was winding up.

"Martin, I know what you're thinking."

"Damn right, you do!" I moved over to her slowly, the spring tightening. The old guy was dead. That's all could think of. He wouldn't be getting that year or two of peace he wanted. So little, so damn little.

"Martin—" She tried to back away. I grabbed her.

"How was it done, Joyce?" I turned her around, twisting her arm behind her in a hammer lock.

"Tell me how it was done, Joyce!" I bent her over the desk, still holding the hammer lock, pushing it higher until her arm was folded up tight between her shoulder blades.

"Martin, my arm!"

She started to scream. I let up a bit.

"Your last chance, Joyce. Tell me how it was done or I'll break it. So help me God, I'll break it and let you do the explaining later."

"My arm, my arm!"

I reached over, clamped my hand over her mouth, turned it on then, pushing her arm higher. I was ready to break it. I *wanted* to.

"Last chance, Joyce."

I let up on the pressure and took my hand from her mouth. She gasped for air.

"Martin, you don't under— *all right, all right, I did it!* My arm, Martin, my arm! Oh, God!"

"How?"

"The pills."

I let go of her arm and backed away. She straightened and turned, the arm falling limply at her side. Tears of pain were in her eyes.

"It was for you, Martin. For you and me. He was still going to fire—"

The slap caught her high on the cheek. She stumbled away from the desk. I followed her, grabbed the neck of her robe to hold her upright. I slapped her again.

"Martin—"

I followed her across the room, putting my weight behind each slap, then backhanding her. Her head bounced from side to side.

"Martin, my God!" She covered her reddened face with her arm, backing against the bulkhead, unable to move further. She kept her arms about her face.

"Martin, you don't know what you're—"

Her robe was open. I caught the neck of her pajamas and ripped down. Her hands dropped to cover herself and I slapped her again. I couldn't stop. I wanted to kill her.

When she covered her face again I stepped in

close, jamming my fist into her soft white belly, not hard, not gently; enough so she'd never forget it. She doubled over, retching, holding her belly, coughing as if she had something in her throat.

I stood there trembling, fighting to control myself. My hands kept opening and closing. Suddenly she slumped down to her knees and began crying. Both sides of her flaming face were puffing up.

The fight went out of me then, and I felt a little weak, a little sick. I went over and got the glass of brandy I'd poured before and sat down behind the desk. I watched her dabbing at her eyes, pushing her disheveled hair from her face.

I finished the brandy, then poured another. That was half gone before she got up from her knees and went over to the washstand. She used a towel to bathe her face, her reddened eyes catching mine occasionally in the mirror. She looked a mess.

I began to feel sorry for her. She'd be paying for the old man's death the rest of her life. Who was I to add to the payment?

"You might even hang for this, Joyce."

She put the towel down and turned. "I'm willing to forget what just happened because I know I deserved it. But if you touch me again, Martin, I'll scream for help. I'm not going to take it again."

"I'm not going to touch you. You'll be paying later."

"I don't think so."

She looked across the room at me levelly. There was a small cut on her lower lip and a little blood on her robe.

"I don't think it's going to work out the way you think, Martin. Can I talk to you calmly, without you getting rough again?"

"Talk away."

She went over and sat in the leather chair. "May I have a cigarette?"

I threw her the pack.

She lit one up, inhaled, and let the smoke trickle from her nostrils.

"I don't intend to hang, Martin, or anything *like* that. There is no proof that Ezra's passing was caused by anything but old age."

"Better wake up, Joyce. In this day and age we have autopsies."

"But we're not going to have an autopsy."

"That's what *you* think. I'm putting that body ashore in Shanghai for a medical report. Then we'll have it embalmed and taken to the States."

She nodded. "And what do you think the autopsy will show?"

"You tell me."

"An overdose of the tablets he used every night."

"That's enough for any board of inquiry. They'll hang you."

"Not if Ezra Sloan committed suicide."

I stared over at her. "What makes you think that will stick?"

She stared right back. "What makes you think it won't? Is there any proof he died differently?"

"Joyce, you're off your rocker. The old guy wouldn't commit suicide. No reason."

"Of course he had reasons. He was despondent over his health, and about us. He was driven to it, Martin, when he found out his wife and employee were having an affair." She didn't bat an eyelash. The smoke trickled from her nostrils.

"That's your story, eh?"

"Can you think of a better one?" She drew on the cigarette again. "But it won't be necessary for any board of inquiry to stick their noses into this, Martin. You're going to give my husband a sea burial and not an autopsy. Shall I tell you why?"

"Please do."

"Then listen: At any board of inquiry where there

is doubt as to the cause of death, witnesses testify, giving all information they know of that would have any bearing. At this particular inquiry—if you insist on having one—I will testify that my husband committed suicide, that I believe our affair aboard ship caused it. The crew will have to testify as to what they know, and their testimony will leave little doubt of our indiscretions—especially if I, a woman, am quite frank about it. Without definite proof that Ezra didn't commit suicide, I'll go scot free. Disgraced by the newspaper publicity, perhaps, but free."

"Wishful thinking, Joyce." I wondered if it was. She had an out. No doubt about it.

"I'll go free, Martin, and you know it. But I didn't tell you the reason why you'll agree with me that Ezra should be buried at sea, and as soon as possible. Have you thought of your name in shipping when it's brought out that my husband may have been driven to suicide by *your* actions? Have you thought of *that* part of it, of your chances of getting a berth after the headlines in the San Francisco newspapers? And it's always headlines where sex is concerned, isn't it, Martin? And isn't it a federal offense for any ship's officer to step out of line with a female of passenger status? Martin, tell me something: What will your license be worth after an inquiry into the death of Ezra Sloan?"

I got up and kicked back the chair.

She eyed me coldly. "Sit down, Martin. Sit down or I'll start screaming and we won't have any choice *but* an inquiry. Nothing will ever make me say Ezra didn't commit suicide. *Nothing.* That will be my story and *you'll* be stuck with it."

I wanted to go over and kick her teeth out. I wanted to go over and start in where I'd left off. But I didn't. A dozen pictures flickered in my mind. As if a projector were flashing them one by one, I saw the inquiry, the newspapers, the story on everyone's lips. I even saw the gray walls of a prison if her passenger status was accepted by the steamboat inspectors.

I sat down again.

She leaned forward. "But it's an easy choice, Martin. Scandal and disgrace on the one hand; on the other, your job secured for as long as you wish." She touched her cheek and winced. "Another woman would be furious with you, but I'm not. I almost welcomed that beating. It's like punishment, in a way. I feel better for it."

I got up and put on my coat.

Her eyes followed me to the door, "I wouldn't do anything foolish, Martin. Remember, you can ruin yourself but not me. Without definite proof I'll go free. Can you offer any reason why I'd want Ezra out of the way? Reasons that wouldn't sound silly? After all, this ship would be mine in a few years at the most. Would you tell them I did it for you?"

I slammed the door behind me and went out on the well deck. Spray was whipping over the dark decks but I stood at the rail welcoming the cold sting of it, cursing Joyce and then myself for not having the guts to charge her with murder.

But it takes more than a charge to make murder stick, and I didn't have the slightest bit of evidence to offer. Once the charge was made, proof would be asked for, and—the motive. There wasn't any proof. How about the motive? She was right that the true one would sound silly. Sloan was an old man and she wouldn't have too long a wait to inherit the vessel, so what other reasons could she have for murder? Big handsome me? I could just see the tough skippers on the board of inquiry taking a good look at my pan, being asked to believe this was the guy she murdered for. Oh, brother.

She'd go free, all right. I saw that, clearly. I saw something else, too: the charges being made out against me. My ticket could be hung in a ship's head for all the use it would be after a public hearing.

I walked down the deck, thinking it out. If Sloan were buried at sea he would be just an old skipper who had passed away in his sleep, just as Joyce said. No investigations, no inquiry. Just a single report to the inspectors for their records. The choice was mine. I could make a big thing out of it, or keep my mouth shut.

What would it cost to play it her way? My conscience? Sloan was gone. I couldn't bring him back by being a fall guy. I was very much alive and had Lewandowski to watch out for.

Sloan died in his sleep. I'd think of it that way. I'd keep thinking along that line. Maybe I'd get to believe it.

"Evenin', Cap."

I almost bumped into the second assistant. He stood at the engine-room hatch wiping the sweat from his grimy neck with a piece of waste.

I tried to sound natural.

"Good evening, Gaynor. How's everything below?"

"Tiptop, Cap. Bit hot, though."

"Guess it is. That ventilation system working any better?"

He lifted his heavy shoulders. "So-so. The intake's bad. Smokes so much we keep shutting it down."

"Any scoops out?"

"Didn't know we had any."

"I'll have Phelps rig some in the morning."

"Be fine, Cap. A help."

"Good night, Gaynor."

"Night, Cap."

She was inspecting the bruises on her face when I came in. I took off my coat, poured myself a drink, and lit a cigarette.

"Do I look any better, Martin?"

"You should look worse. I stopped too soon."

"That kind of talk won't get us anywhere."

"I want you to answer some questions: How many pills did you use?"

She looked at me suspiciously. "Why do you want to know that?"

"Damnit, answer the question! Once this ball is rolling I want nothing stupid tripping us."

"Oh, I see.... Thirteen."

"How did you get them?"

She fooled with her fingers, examining her nails. "I saved them from his old bottles. He got a fresh bottle of one hundred each time we left the States and he hadn't always finished with the old bottle."

"Where is the bottle he's been using now?"

"On his desk."

"How many are in it?"

"About ... No, it's the full one. Just one missing. He had just finished with the old one the night before."

"O.K., that's a break. When you go back there, leave it on the desk in plain view. Anyone seeing it will think the obvious, that if only one is missing it wasn't the cause of death. Incidentally, how did you get him to take so many pills?"

"I put them in his milk, stirring them well. Oh, you mean the taste? I put brandy in the milk to make it good and bitter."

"Thought he didn't like the taste of brandy."

"He took it with a little coaxing."

"What'd you do, pat his cheek and love him up a bit? Nursie knows best?"

Her face hardened. "Martin, I don't like that kind of talk."

"You don't, eh? How do you think I like it?"

"I don't know why you're so upset. You had nothing do with anything."

"Yeah, that makes me feel good. Now listen: I just

met Gaynor on deck. We talked. That means we'll have to play it that Sloan didn't pass away yet. Gaynor would think it damn funny I'm out strolling an hour after Sloan died and didn't even bother mentioning the fact. You go back in the cabin, put some make-up on, then call Phelps down from the bridge. How did you discover your husband was dead?"

"What? Oh, I went to him— No, let's see.... He called and I went to him." She looked at me. "That's it: I heard him call."

"You *thought* you heard him call. You went to him, he wasn't breathing. O.K., get in there. Don't forget to change your robe. And listen, don't act too weepy. Phelps knows why you married Sloan, so don't ham it up. Any questions?"

"No. I don't think so." She put her hands gingerly to her cheeks. "What will Phelps think of the way I look?"

"Keep your face down into a handkerchief. Tomorrow, wear a veil. Got one?"

"I have a black one."

"Thought of everything, didn't you?"

"I said before, Martin, that kind of talk won't get us anywhere."

"When you call Phelps, make it loud. Enough to wake me."

"You won't leave me alone with him too long, will you?"

"Three minutes and I'll be in there. I want nobody touching that body. Drum it into your head that he went off in his sleep and act exactly as if he did. Tomorrow morning he'll be over the side and the devil himself couldn't say he didn't die in his sleep."

"Will a half hour from now be all right? I want to freshen up."

"O.K., but no longer than that." I went over to the bureau and got the brandy again.

"Martin, you shouldn't drink so much."

"You keep that busy little brain of yours on your own problems and don't worry about my drinking."

She still didn't go. "When it's all over, Martin, everything will be all right, won't it? Between us, I mean?" She gave me a tentative smile.

"Sure, everything will be great! After the crew has a look-see and leaves the cabin we'll hold hands over the body the rest of the night."

When she went out the door I felt like heaving the bottle after her.

I kicked off my shoes and stretched out on the bunk. Two bells sounded. One A.M. I closed my eyes, listening to the dissolving tones of the bell, the throb of the Diesels, the slap of the rising sea against the side of the ship. A lot depended on Joyce's actions when Phelps came down from the bridge. It had to be smooth from start to finish. No rough edges. Phelps would be on the scene plenty dazed, sure, but every move that Joyce and I made must fall naturally into place, every gesture and word the proper one, befitting a simple death from natural causes. I tried to visualize the scene in the cabin when I would make my entrance. She'd be in her pajamas, wearing a robe....

I sat straight up, the question bouncing into my head: Would you grab a robe after finding your husband dead in bed? Some women would, but would Joyce? Was she the type? Not that baby. At least, not for the sake of modesty. And maybe Phelps would think about that.

I got up and lit a cigarette, trying to convince myself the robe was unimportant. The clock on the wall said one-fifteen.

That robe. That damned robe.

I started pacing the floor and two cigarettes later had almost convinced myself that Phelps knew nothing about women or what they'd be likely to wear, so what was I worried about?

I tossed the cigarette out the port and looked at the clock. It read one-forty. What the hell could she be doing?

That's when I started sweating. Suppose she couldn't call Phelps? Suppose she was in there now, sweating it out, unable to go on with it? Or maybe she'd go hysterical when Phelps came down, blabber out the whole story with me right in the middle of it.

"Mr. Ph-Phelps! Mr. Phelps! Hurry, please...." Her voice trailed off, stuttering incoherently.

I wiped the sweat off my face and neck with a towel, changed my undershirt, and put on trousers and slippers.

That took about three minutes.

I walked up the passageway to the cabin with little butterflies racing up my spine.

She didn't have on a robe, or pajamas either. It was a pale blue nightgown, sheer. Much better. Diverting. Whether she was actually crying or not I didn't know, but her head was buried in Phelps' shoulder and he was awkwardly holding her, looking embarrassed, wondering where to put his hands.

He saw me and tilted his head nervously toward the inner stateroom. "Terrible, Captain. Just terrible."

I went into the other room. A patchwork quilt was drawn up to Sloan's chin. His arms were outside the quilt. His eyes were closed, his lips parted. The subdued light from the bed lamp shaded the scarring on his face. He looked peaceful and relaxed, exactly like a man who had passed away in his sleep.

Which, in a way, he had.

It didn't bother me too much looking down at Sloan. I was sorry for him, sure, but now I had plenty on my mind. I had Lewandowski to think about.

I turned and watched Phelps helping Joyce into the room, over to her bed. He was gently patting her shoulder, his forehead clouded with the effort of searching for an appropriate word. "Mrs. Sloan, please ... please now.... Now, Mrs. Sloan, you must control yourself. Really you must." He looked over at me helplessly as she continued to cling to him.

If she was acting, she was certainly starting to louse it up. "Mrs. Sloan!"

She calmed down a little then, and Phelps managed to free her hands from his neck. She sat down on her bed, her face lowered. She accepted Phelps' handkerchief.

"I'm sorry. It was such a shock. I thought I heard something and got up to go to him. When I t-touched him he was—" She shook her head, as if unable to go on.

Phelps cleared his throat several times, started to say something, then simply patted her shoulder again. He came over and stood beside me, looking down at Sloan.

I wondered if he was taking note of the peaceful expression on Sloan's face, and decided to put in a word of my own in case he wasn't.

"He seems to have passed away easily enough, Phelps. In his sleep, apparently. A good way to go when we have to."

Phelps nodded. He removed his glasses and wiped the lenses. "He was a good man, Captain. Never an unkind word in all the years I've known him. A good man."

"The best."

"Life hadn't been too good to him."

"Perhaps his reward will come in another place." Tall corn, strictly from the Ozarks, but Phelps solemnly nodded.

I bent down to pull the quilt over Sloan's face. It had been tucked in firmly at the foot of the bed and Phelps moved around to free it.

"His hands first, Captain."

"Eh?"

"I think you fold the hands across the chest. It seems to be the thing to do."

It was while I was picking up each limp hand that I saw something that hit me in the stomach with the force of a sledge hammer.

I pulled the quilt up and covered Sloan's face, my hands trembling. I shoved them in my pockets when I straightened. I didn't know what to do. I just didn't know. I needed time to think.

"Phelps, did you leave anybody on the bridge?"

"No, but I think it's all right. The lookout is Walters. He'd have sense enough—"

"We can't take any chances, Phelps. Better go back up there. Have the watch muffle the bell and toll it for one minute, but pass the word for the crew to pay their respects in the morning. Mrs. Sloan will have better control of herself by then."

I heard him mumble something to Joyce that was meant to be comforting. I didn't turn around until the door closed and his heavy step sounded on the ladder leading to the bridge.

She had guessed and was on her feet, the blood draining from her face.

"He can't be alive, Martin! He *can't!*"

The bell outside began tolling.

Chapter Eleven

"Is the door locked?"

"Yes, of course."

"Check it again and make sure."

"But I'm positive."

"You were positive he was dead. Get up and check that door!" We were in the outer room, the decanter of brandy on the table in front of me. I was on my second glass, trying to break the tight feeling in my head.

What would happen when Sloan woke up? He'd be bound to know the score. Would he blame me? Would Joyce decide to let me share the guilt?

She came back from the door and sat down across from me again, still twisting the handkerchief Phelps had given her. "Martin, should you be drinking like this?" She looked ready to cry. "I don't think you should. Really, Martin, I don't think you should."

"Shut up, Joyce."

"But we must do something."

"If I knew what to do I'd be doing it. He's unconscious, so he can't swallow anything to bring the stuff up. Maybe the best thing to do is let him sleep it off. I don't know. We'll wait and see."

She gaped at me. "I didn't mean *that*."

"What *do* you mean?"

"If he lives I'll be in trouble. Terrible trouble. He may not say anything to the police, but he'll put me ashore, divorce me. Or leave the ship to someone else."

"Stop, Joyce, you'll have me in tears. Any more of this stuff in the cabin?"

"Martin, it's not a good idea to keep drinking. You drink too much."

"I asked if there was any more in the cabin."

"No."

"Well, there's plenty in the storeroom. Break out a bottle."

She looked at me nervously. "Martin, we have to talk about ... about him. If you keep drinking—"

"We don't have to talk about anything. I feel like breaking your silly head against the bulkhead, and if you don't produce that bottle I'll get up and do it."

I outstared her. She went over to the buffet.

She came back with the bottle. "Darling, listen—"

"Put it on the table. Right here."

She did, and I was half disappointed. I'd have enjoyed pushing her around again.

"Then you won't do anything, Martin?"

"If you mean I won't shove some more pills down his throat, no. Good God, is there any bottom to the things you can think of? What kind of devil are you, anyway?"

Her eyes had darted over my shoulder. I thought she was going to faint.

I swung around. Sloan was swaying in the doorway, holding himself erect with effort, his eyes closed, his head lolling from side to side. Saliva trickled from his mouth down onto his pajamas.

He looked like a drunk ready to pass out.

"Take him back to bed, Martin!" She was breathing hard, choking out the words. "Martin, he doesn't know where he's at. Take him back ... before I *scream!*"

She stood beside me while I arranged the quilt over Sloan again. He had offered no resistance when I led him back to his bunk, walking the short distance as if in a deep sleep, his eyes closed, his breathing shallow and regular.

"Martin, I'm frightened. Tomorrow he'll head for the nearest port—"

I was still leaning over the bunk, loosening the top button of Sloan's pajamas, when his eyelids fluttered open. He looked straight up at Joyce, his small blue eyes unclouded, his wrinkled mouth moving.

"Joyce ... don't. Don't do it."

Her hand gripped my arm as I tried to step back. "He knows, Martin. He knows. My God, don't just stand there. *Do* something!"

Sloan heard her. He didn't stir a muscle, his body apparently held in the grip of the drug again. But his deep-set eyes betrayed his thoughts, and once again I got the impression of a small child staring from behind a grotesque mask, only this time the child was frightened.

I opened the port above the bunk for air.

"Martin—"

"Shut up and make yourself useful. Get some cold towels while I'm gone and lay them on his head. The medicine chest in my room may have something. As long as he's conscious, maybe we can force an antidote down his throat."

The only suitable wash I could find in the chest was a pound of bicarbonate of soda. Maybe if we could get enough of it into Sloan it might do the trick.

I had to wait in the passageway a few minutes for the lookout relief to go forward, then I went into the cabin.

Joyce was sitting at the table, smoking, studying the bottle of brandy. The light was out in Sloan's room.

"Did you do as I told you? Put wet towels on his head?"

She lifted her eyes and I read the defiance in them. I read something else, and a knot began forming in my stomach.

I went into the inner room and snapped on the bed lamp. Sloan stared up at me, a horrible twisted grin on his mouth. I didn't have to touch him to know he was dead. The pillow that had been taken from under his head was now on the floor. It told the story of how he died; his expression said that being smothered was not an easy way to die.

I couldn't take it.

I just made the bathroom. Everything came up. Everything except that knot. That stayed in my belly, cold and hard.

"If you don't lower your voice someone will hear you. Then where will we be?"

I knew where I wanted to be. At that moment I wanted to be on the beach in Shanghai with three months' pay and passage home. I wanted to be anyplace except on the Trader.

I sat down and took the drink she pushed across the table. I couldn't get over the way she acted, cool and calm, not a care in the world. Apparently the only thing that had upset her before was the fact that Sloan might not have died. He was gone now, so she had no worries.

Everything was fine and dandy.

"Stop staring at me, Martin. It won't do you one bit of good to lose your temper again. Everything is the same as it was before—except we have to straighten Ezra's face, if it can be done."

My stomach churned. I had to gulp the brandy fast to keep it down.

She went on: "In a few hours the crew will be standing outside, waiting to view the body. We'll have to think of some way to prevent that. Phelps would be certain to notice the difference and we'd surely be in trouble." She lit two cigarettes and passed one over to me. Her hand was steady. Mine wasn't.

"I hope, Martin, from this point on you get a grip on yourself and act sensibly. If you don't, and we're caught, everybody will say you're as guilty as I am."

That's what hurt. I was in this thing right up to my neck and I knew it. It was a case of playing along all the way or sticking that neck in a noose. Whether I wanted to or not, I had to carry this ball—and do it with a clear head, without arguing or fighting with Joyce.

"It's exactly the same as before, Martin. You see that, don't you?"

The knock on the door brought me out of the chair. "Don't open it. Just find out what he wants."

She moved over to the door. "Yes? Who is it?" Her voice was level, well under control.

"Walters, ma'am. Is the skipper there?"

She looked over at me. I nodded. She opened the door a crack. "Yes, Walters?"

"Gerlack is feelin' bad, ma'am, and Mr. Garrett'd

like to have the Captain look him over. Sure hate to bother you at a time like this, but the skipper wasn't in his room and I thought—"

"He's in here, Walters. Helping me to dress my husband."

I almost gagged at the thought of it.

"I'll let him know about Gerlack and he'll be there in about five minutes. Is that all right?"

"Yes'm." Walters cleared his throat. "Me an' the boys are sorry for your troubles, ma'am. Anything we can do, you just say the word."

"Thank you, Walters. You're very kind."

She closed the door. I went over to the sink and splashed water on my face.

"Feeling better now?" She handed me a towel.

I wanted to knock that complacent look from her face but had sense enough not to start anything.

Sloan died in his sleep. Sloan died in his sleep....

"I'm O.K. I'll have to go forward and take a look at Gerlack. They'll be expecting me."

"If any of the men ask when they can see the body, what will you tell them?"

"I'll think of something. Don't let anybody in until I get back."

"Suppose Ferguson and Phelps object in the morning to giving Ezra a sea burial? They both know he wished to be buried ashore."

"We'll cross that when we come to it."

Gerlack was in his drawers, lying on a lower bunk. In the feeble compartment light his body looked hot and dry. There were blotches on his belly. Garrett was sitting at the foot of the bunk, squinting at a thermometer.

A few seamen were standing around, half dressed, smoking, yawning.

"Looks a little like measles, Martin."

"Ain't that. I had 'em." Gerlack's tongue was

thick, his speech slurred. Some wiseacre pulled the old one about he got more than he paid for at Chefoo. It got a laugh.

I bent over and pulled his eyelids back. His eyes were red and watery, but free of pus.

"How long have you had this thing?"

"Hit me bad tonight, Cap. Woke up feeling like a fried spud."

"I mean how long have you been walking around with a fever and these spots?"

"Three, four days. Maybe since leaving Shanghai."

"You're a blockhead, Gerlack. Did you stop to consider you're mingling with twenty men and could be passing something along? Open your mouth."

His tongue was furred, and along the mucous membrane were some faint spots, purplish in color. Measles, all right. Another day or two and his face would blossom out.

Gerlack closed his mouth and waited anxiously for the verdict. Reflected in his feverish eyes was the seaman's dread of shipboard sicknesses after leaving foreign ports. That's what gave me the idea, his deep concern, that and the circular blue-black bruise on his chest.

I inspected the bruise, stalling for time. There was nothing unusual about the bruise except its almost perfect circular shape, but the gimmick *might* work. No reason why it shouldn't. If it didn't, nothing would be lost.

I stood up and looked at the deckies standing about, none of them too interested, all a little annoyed that they were losing sleep.

"Have you ever seen the plague start like this, Pappy?"

The silence was like an explosion. The sleepiness was wiped off all faces and they gaped at me with but one expression: fear. On a ship at sea not even a fire can compete with the terrible feeling the word "plague" brings on.

Garrett rose from the bunk, shaking his head, the only one not convinced.

"I don't know, Martin. Never run into the plague, but it seems to me this is a kid's disease. Like the measles. At the worst I figured it might be typhus."

"Maybe, Pappy, maybe. But while I was dressing Sloan I noticed a swelling at his groin. And I didn't like the color of his skin. Small blotches of black here and there. Like bruises. Similar to the one on Gerlack's chest."

All eyes swung to Gerlack. He was staring up at me, thoroughly frightened. Apparently he'd forgotten where the bruise came from.

Even Garrett looked uneasy now. "Well, there's no telling about these things."

"I'm not saying Sloan *had* the plague, Pappy, but I can't guarantee he hadn't. He wasn't a well man and the preliminary stages of something like that could've finished him before it became too apparent. I think I've got it   a touch of something myself, so we may have the bug aboard."

The man nearest me moved away a trifle, then looked ashamed. Suddenly I felt better, two worries off my mind. No one would be viewing Sloan's body now, and any objection to disposing of it over the side could easily be overruled without creating suspicion.

"I don't want to alarm you men unduly, but we'll treat this case as if it *were* the plague. We'll take no chances. Gerlack will be moved into a spare room on the port side. He'll be under quarantine until this thing clears up. First thing in the morning I want this compartment cleaned out and scrubbed down, Gerlack's bedding and bunk taken topside and jettisoned. There'll be no work performed after that, except the watches, of course. I want every man to take it as easy as possible, staying well rested. And keep away from that coolie gang in the fantail. We'll rope that off tonight."

I turned to the carpenter standing to one side, buttoning his trousers. "Peterson, can you make a burial bag by morning for the old man's body?"

"I think so, sir. I ..." A funny look came into his eyes.

"It's all right. You won't have to touch the body. Leave the bag at the cabin door. I'll take care of it myself."

He looked relieved.

"How do the rest of you men feel? Anybody feeling out of sorts, warm, uncomfortable?"

They looked uncertain, as I knew they would. Aboard a freighter at sea the man who wasn't uncomfortable or warm after plague is mentioned has more stomach than brains.

"Pappy, go aft and check on the black gang. Anybody not feeling well put in with Gerlack. Better speak to each man personally, look him over good. Especially for swellings under the arms or near the groin."

I left the compartment feeling well satisfied, my head clearer. After Garrett made the rounds there wouldn't be a man aboard who wouldn't be sick from fear alone. They'd be so busy sticking their tongues at mirrors they wouldn't be giving a second thought to Sloan.

When I walked in she was pinning her hair back in an upsweep. She wore a long powder-blue evening gown, strapless, a gold rope belt around her waist.

"Hello, darling. Like me?" She whirled on her high heels and her dress flared out over solid thighs and black lace panties.

"What the devil do you call this?"

"A new dress I bought in Shanghai."

"Are you going nuts? Lights on and trying on an evening gown at a time like this! Good God, Joyce, you're the limit."

"Nobody ever walks in without knocking, Martin, so please calm down."

"Oh, brother!"

"I've been busy while you've been gone. He looks much better now."

"Who looks better?"

"Ezra. I fixed his face while you were forward."

I stared at her. "Doesn't anything ever bother you?"

"Do you think I relished the job? It was simply something that had to be done."

I gave her a rundown of the general reaction to the mention of plague.

"Martin, that *was* clever."

"You oppose his burial in the morning."

"I oppose— Oh, yes, of course."

"Be firm about it. He requested burial ashore and that's the way you want it."

"I'll remember."

"I'll be just as stubborn for dumping him immediately. Won't do any harm to let them hear us argue a bit. Do a lot of good, in fact."

"Martin, we're doing all right."

I gave her a look. "You don't have to be so damn gay about it."

"But we *are*. And you look better, like your old self. I can hardly wait for morning. Then it will be all over with. I know I'll never be able to sleep tonight. Will you?"

"Hardly."

"We'll keep each other company."

I gave her another look. She smiled a little and unhooked the gold belt from her waist. "I *am* rather nice company, don't you think?"

"What the hell have you got in mind?"

"Now, I like that. Did I say anything?"

"You don't have to."

"But I'm just changing my dress."

I closed the door on the rest of it, and went out on deck. I met Garrett coming from the bridge.

"Thought I'd go in and say a proper word, Martin."

"Not tonight, Pappy. She's pretty upset. The shock of it, I guess."

"Well, maybe I'll wait till morning."

"Make it after the funeral. She'll feel a bit better then. Night, Pappy, I'm turning in."

She wouldn't be the only one feeling better after that funeral.

Chapter Twelve

"I insist my husband's wishes be carried out, Captain."

"You can insist all you want to, Mrs. Sloan, but the health of this crew is my first responsibility. With Gerlack still running a temperature, it's my duty to take every precaution against what may be a highly contagious disease. I'm taking no chances. None at all."

"Surely there is some way to keep the body? Store it so there'll be no chance of contact?"

"I've already explained we haven't the facilities for cold storage, and even if we had, I wouldn't like the prospect of carrying a question mark as big as the plague. I'm sorry, but, it's out of the question. Under the circumstances, over the side is a necessary precaution."

We were out on the well deck. Phelps, Ferguson, and a dozen hands were standing around watching the carpenter fashion a table to be used as a chute. The body was by the hatch, bagged and weighted, a tarp covering it. Services were at nine.

Ferguson had been keeping an ear on the conversation, as had the others on deck. He came over, frowning at the bowl of his pipe, obviously not too anxious to butt in. "Maybe we could rig an auxiliary off the ice plant? Build a compartment alongside and lead a coil in there?"

I had been prepared for this one, and gave it some thought, as if it might be an idea, at that. "That would mean carrying it right next to our supplies."

He hesitated. "If it was sealed off—"

"You'd still need coil openings. No, I can't permit it. I'd like to satisfy Mrs. Sloan, but just think how the crew would feel every time a meal was placed in front of them."

I could feel the relief of the men at my firmness. Sloan had been a nice guy, sure, and they'd have felt better knowing he was being buried where he wished. But they were on edge concerning Gerlack's illness, and the sooner Sloan went over the side, the better they'd like it.

Joyce continued to object until I finally turned and walked away. I wanted to leave the impression that anything that might have been between us was now washed up.

Not that it wasn't.

Officers and men stood bareheaded while I read the burial rites from a seaman's Bible. The coolie gang aft were craning their necks for a better view, most of them grinning, quite happy about the whole thing. Being restricted to the fantail until we reached Shanghai meant no work, and that made none of them mad.

With the sky a gray wind-blown canopy and sheets of spray continually shooting across the well deck, I gave it the grand play, taking it slow and easy, lifting my eyes occasionally to the table placed against the bulwark. Four deck hands were standing by the table, two on each side, waiting for my signal to lift and tilt it. A flag covered the body bag, the end of it secured on the inboard side so that when the table was tilted and the body slid off, the flag would remain.

I had timed the rites at better than fifteen minutes that morning, and before half the time had elapsed more than one man was throwing an impatient look my way. They wanted it over and done with. With the cold spray flying across the deck every few seconds, I didn't blame them, but I was in no hurry. When a man is involved in murder he might be in a hurry to dispose of the body. This was one funeral every man would remember as a long solemn service conducted by Captain Lewandowski.

Just in case they might be asked.

Joyce stood beside me, her head bowed, hands clasping a prayer book. Several times during the reading she muffled a sob and I paused each time to punctuate it. By the time I had closed the book everyone was soaked to the skin and all hands were shifting from one foot to the other. But I wasn't finished yet.

I cleared my throat and started the eulogy by touching on Sloan's physical handicaps and the lightness he made of them while inwardly grieving. I spoke of his good-naturedness and his concern for the welfare of the crew, dwelling on the personal interest he took in each individual while he was able to get around. All the slush I could think of I tossed in, and it must have sounded pretty good, because Phelps started wiping his glasses and even Ferguson went fumbling in his pockets for a handkerchief.

When I figured the spiel was just about milked dry, I nodded to the men at the table.

They braced themselves against the roll of the ship and picked it up, the two inboard men tilting it high.

The body wouldn't slide.

The men looked at one another. They shook the table. The canvas bag held fast. They looked back at me uneasily. The Italian was supporting the inboard side and he freed one hand to cross himself.

Even dead, Sloan was refusing a sea burial.

"Tilt it higher." My voice broke but I don't think anybody noticed. All hands were ogling the board, now tilted at a forty-five-degree angle, with Sloan stubbornly hanging on. I heard Joyce say, "Oh, my God," and it was Garrett who walked over and folded back the flag, put his hand under the bag, and lifted.

It slid off and disappeared over the side.

Joyce turned and walked away, her face stiff and chalk white. I went over to the table, where Garrett and the carpenter were inspecting the planking. It was tongue-and-groove stuff with two supporting pieces nailed beneath it. One of the nails, although angled in, had hit a knot and came through on the finished side.

The carpenter was scratching his head. "Sure sorry about this, Cap. It was a quick job and I didn't notice that nail."

I felt like hanging one on his chin. "It's all right, Peterson. These things will happen."

"Don't you think it's about time you stopped going out of your way to avoid me?"

I didn't answer her but kept the glasses trained on the misty blur ahead.

"Martin, I said—"

"Joyce, I don't want you on the bridge. Not during my watch." I put the glasses down and went into the wheelhouse.

Peterson was behind the wheel.

"Come right five."

"Aye, sir." He pushed the spokes past his chest.

I poured some coffee, glancing out on the port wing to see if she'd gone below. She hadn't. She was huddled against the rail, pulling her slicker collar closer to her face against the damp night wind.

Forty-eight hours had passed since the funeral, and I was having a tough job convincing her we were through. That it was strictly business from here on in.

"Bring it back. Steady it."

"Aye, sir. One-eighty-two."

"Make it eighty-one."

I went back outside, into the starboard wing. Through the glasses I saw that the blur ahead was a junk, running as usual without lights.

"Martin, I want to talk to you. I must."

"Is it important, or just talk?"

"It's important."

"Go up on the flying bridge. I'll join you in a few minutes."

I went back in the wheelhouse, finished the coffee, and lit a cigarette.

"Never learn, do they, sir?"

I shot Peterson a look. He got flustered. "I mean the junk, sir. They never learn about lights. They don't seem to worry one bit about being run down."

"That's right, they don't worry. Good reason, too. They know damn well freighters keep a sharp eye in these waters and will give them a wide berth. Those twelve-by-twelves on her bow would open us up like a battering ram butting a sheet-metal door."

I smoked another cigarette, waiting for the junk to be safely bearing to our left, then went topside.

She gave me an impatient look. "That was a long few minutes."

"What's on your mind?"

"You are. The way you're acting. Is there any reason we can't get together occasionally and talk out our problems sensibly?"

"Didn't know we had any problems. I've told you a dozen times everything is O.K., that we don't even have to talk about it. The less talk, the better. Nobody knows anything and they won't know as long as they're not told."

"Martin, you're overlooking one small detail. No one knows about—about it, that's true. No one except us."

"So?"

She caught the rail for balance as the ship rolled. "So it's almost impossible to feel comfortable as long as you treat me like a leper. I have no way of knowing what's going on in your mind, whether you're thinking of ... well, confessing."

"Think I'm nuts? I don't feel like committing suicide, and that's what it would be."

"Well, I don't mean that kind of confession. Perhaps you'll be drinking sometime and talk about it."

"Fat chance. Listen, Joyce, get this straight. The minute that body went over the side I became as guilty as you. Doesn't make the slightest bit of difference that I had nothing to do with his dying. I'm in this, right up to my ears, and all I want to do is forget it ever happened. Suppose you do the same."

"I can't, Martin. It's preying on my mind. I won't feel secure until ..." She hesitated and looked away. "I won't feel secure until we're married."

I stared at her. "What gave you the idea we're going to be married?"

She shrugged and continued looking out into the night. "It's the only safe way for both of us. We can be married secretly in one of those missions outside Shanghai. No one need know for six months, say, and then—"

"You can drop that idea! I'm as close to you now as I ever intend to be."

She wheeled suddenly, her eyes darkening. "No need to be insulting about it!"

"I'm not being insulting. I'm just telling you the score."

"Lower your voice, please. You needn't shout

at—" She broke off, dropped her voice. "Silva. Behind you."

He was standing at the head of the ladder, his big sloppy figure in dirty whites, the flash of his teeth visible in the darkness. He was holding a tray in his hands, two cups on it.

"Hot coffee, Captain, sir, for you and for the lady."

He made a little bow. "One thing I never do is neglect the small comforts. No sense in being boss man, I always say, if you can't have the little privileges that go with—"

"Since when did you start bringing coffee up on my watch?" I walked over to him slowly. He held the tray out, his fleshy face managing to crease with surprise and still hold the grin.

"Well, Captain, the night is rather cool and it came to me suddenly you'd appreciate—"

"I hadn't noticed it was any cooler tonight than other nights. Besides, a thermos of coffee is kept in the chartroom for the officers. You know it as well as I do."

His dark eyes moved over my shoulder to Joyce. "But this is fresh coffee, sir, and since there was a lady up here—"

"Why didn't you leave it below, in the wheelhouse?"

"Shall I leave it there now, sir? I thought—"

"Answer my question, Silva. Why didn't you leave the coffee—" I stopped short. Why make an issue of it? "Yes, do that, Silva. In the future, when you have occasion to come to the bridge with coffee, leave it down in the wheelhouse."

I turned my back on him and went over to the rail again. Below came the sound of the wheelhouse door closing. She let out her breath slowly. "Martin, I'm afraid."

"He heard nothing."

"I'm still afraid."

"Forget it. I said he heard nothing."

"But why did he come up here?"

"To nosy around, but with nothing like you're thinking in mind. Maybe he expected to see a clinch, a little loving, something he could chew over later in the fo'c'sle."

"I've always been a little afraid of that man. He seems so irresponsible, as if he'd never be afraid to do anything. I know he takes a delight in being feared. When he first came aboard, the men complained to Ezra that he had a habit of getting up in the middle of the night and sharpening that knife he always carries, muttering he was going to get even with someone. Nobody would sleep the rest of the night, of course, because each man would lie awake and wonder if Silva meant him."

"If I ever hear any complaints like that I'll drop Mr. Silva off at the nearest port. And I won't even bother running out the gangway."

"Oh, he doesn't do it anymore. Ezra saw to that. There's one story they tell about him, though, that makes me shiver just to think of it. The time he was employed aboard a Greek ship. Ever hear about it?"

I didn't care to listen to sea stories, which were generally 90 per cent imagination, but since Garrett had also spoken of it I shook my head and told her to go on.

"It's really gruesome. They say some of the men on the Greek ship were teasing Silva, telling him he had no real courage, that he only carried his knife to show off. They told him he'd have to bring a Chinaman's ear back aboard before they'd believe he really would use it."

"And I suppose he brought one back."

"*Two*, not one. He's supposed to have brought back two ears in a paper bag, with the earrings still attached to them."

"A long time ago, Joyce, I stopped believing everything I heard in the fo'c'sle, and I'd advise you to do the same. Listen, I have some work to do in the chartroom. Be a good idea in the future to stop these confabs on the bridge. Doesn't look good. If we have any talking to do, it's best to do it in the open, on deck, in daylight."

"But we haven't settled everything yet, Martin." She took out some cigarettes and offered me one.

I shook my head and kept looking at her. "Marriage is out, Joyce. I've made up my mind to that."

"I have too. Made up my mind." She lit her cigarette and looked at me with the smoke dribbling from her nostrils, a sight I was beginning to hate. "I'd never be able to rest easy knowing a word from you could mean trouble for me. I'd worry about that, Martin, and I hate to worry. We must be tied together so neither of us will ever have anything to gain by hurting the other. Otherwise, I can easily see myself going to the police as soon as we reach port and asking that my husband's death be investigated."

She tilted her head, questioning. "See my point, Martin? I'd attempt to settle the case as suicide, once and for all. But even if a verdict couldn't be reached, *you* would be discredited as a ship's officer. I'd have to do that, you see, so that if you ever did say anything about the way Ezra died, it would be put down to mere revenge against the woman who ruined you."

I had all I could do to keep my hands still. "Joyce, your reasoning is lousy. It would be a crazy thing, bringing the case up just to blacken me. There's not the slightest possibility of my ever blabbing."

"Just because *you* say so? I'm sorry, Martin, but there's too much at stake. I'll be satisfied with nothing less than being married."

At that moment I hated her so much I couldn't

speak. I turned and walked away.

Five bells were being struck when I swept the first empty onto the floor. It didn't break. I opened another bottle.

She held the reins with that suicide angle, all right. The laughable part of it was that she couldn't be hurt by asking for an inquiry on Sloan's death, and I could. When the dirt started flying, plenty of it would stick on both of us, but she would have the Trader as consolation; I'd have a worthless ticket.

Even if I wanted to play it stupid and spill the truth, it was a thousand to one against her being convicted. It was my word against hers. And the first thing they'd think was that I was trying to clear my name at her expense without thinking of the consequences.

I got up for some cigarettes and almost staggered. O.K., I'd get slopped up and forget the whole mess for a while. She wanted to get married, eh? Well, why not? Half the Trader would be mine then.

Garrett came in, stopping short when he saw the bottles on the floor. The second one had broken.

"Well, well. What's this?" He gave me a smile.

"What'd you want?"

"Just thought I'd come in and see—"

"Well, get out and stop your damn snooping!" He clucked with his tongue. "Now, now, lad—"

"Don't 'now, now' me! You knock on that door next time. 'Bout time I had some privacy around here. G'wan, get out!"

The lines around his mouth tightened. "Just came down to call you for your watch."

"You do the watch! Let Phelps do it! Put Silva on watch. Who gives a damn? Now get out and don't come back!"

Chapter Thirteen

We were married in a small village some twenty miles outside Shanghai. A fat, raw-faced missionary faintly smelling of liquor did the job, gave Joyce a wet-sounding kiss, and shook my hand.

"Nice-looking girl, Captain. Indeed she is. Yes, indeed. Reminds me of my own wife, may the Lord rest her soul. Sweet woman, she was, indeed she was. A worker, you'd call her. Never complaining. Never a word against the poor lot of those who choose to walk with God... Eh? Why, thank you, Captain, thank you! Not necessary, you know. Not at all. But your generosity will go to help the unfortunate."

"Is there any place we can get a decent meal around here?"

"Indeed there is. Indeed there is...." He shooed away the two grinning Chinese girls who had acted as witnesses and led me over to a window. He jabbed a fat finger at the dusty road converging in the distance on a cluster of pagoda roofs. A small lake shimmered in the background.

"The end establishment, Captain, caters to the few Occidentals who pass this way. Right before you come to the lake. Think you'll be satisfied. Try their chicken baskets and wine. Both excellent."

I thanked him, picked up Joyce's overnight bag, and took her arm going down the stone steps. The missionary trailed behind us, still chattering away, waxing lyrical on the way Joyce looked.

She did look good, at that. She wore a white linen suit, a tight green sweater under the jacket that accented everything she carried. Her dark hair was swept back under a green bandanna and her cheeks were flushed. Her eyes sparkled whenever she smiled. And she was smiling plenty, quite happy about the whole thing.

I couldn't get over the lovey-dovey attitude after I'd agreed to the marriage proposition. Maybe she figured on setting an example on how to make the best of things, or maybe she figured on trying to right things between us, bring them back to where they were before Sloan's death. Whatever it was, nothing had been too good for Martin dear from the time I went into the cabin to give my O.K. She'd fluttered around the room, bringing out wine and cake, and then breaking out a half-dozen dresses to see which I would like for the ceremony. I didn't give a damn but picked the linen suit, and then she brought out the Trader's strongbox, counted out a thousand dollars, and shoved it into my pocket for expenses.

"Martin, I guess it's not very nice."

Joyce wrinkled her nose at the "excellent establishment," and I didn't blame her. A frowzy Chinese woman with swollen legs came forward, bowing and grinning, trying at the same time to shoo green flies away from her greasy black hair. The three tables in the dining room also had their quota of flies. A small potbellied kid came out from the kitchen relieving himself on the way out, and this decided things for Joyce. She backed away hastily as the woman tried to show her to a table.

"No, we're not hungry." She looked at me. "Martin, feel hungry?"

"I can eat, but not in here."

"Why don't we order a chicken basket and the wine the missionary spoke about and take them out by the lake? Have a picnic out there by ourselves?"

"Good enough."

The woman rushed away to fill the order and I went outside for a smoke, watching two kids trying to put a raft of bamboo together.

Joyce joined me in a few minutes. "I inspected

their rooms. One didn't seem *too* bad. At least the sheets were clean. I left my bag up there."

"Staying over?"

She didn't say anything for a moment, making a show of being interested in the kids pushing the raft out on the water.

"Martin, let's try hard. Everything is ahead of us if we want it. Can't we try? Just a little?"

"Sure. Why not?"

She turned quickly, her eyes searching mine, looking for the joker.

There was one, all right, but she couldn't see it. It was buried deep in the hatred I had for her. When the right time came she'd see it.

The woman came out with a small basket covered with a napkin, and a bucket holding two bottles of wine. I took the stuff and followed Joyce down to the lake, where the kids were splashing each other. They yelled something to Joyce and she smiled and waved.

We walked along the edge of the lake, away from the kids, until we came to a grassy clearing. "How will this do, Martin?"

"Sure. Nice spot."

She sat down, spread the napkin, and opened the basket. I struggled with the corks on the bottles, finally made it. "No glasses. Drink as is, I guess."

"I don't mind, really. It feels more like a picnic this way."

The chicken wasn't bad and neither was the wine. We finished most of it and Joyce stretched out flat on her stomach with a sigh of contentment, gazing across the lake at the line of cypresses bowing down at their reflections in the water.

"Just look at those trees, Martin. Aren't they pretty? You forget there are places like this ashore. So restful and quiet. No motion or sound except for a gentle breeze. Martin, let's do this often. Leave the ship, I mean, on little holidays. Perhaps we could even miss a trip or two, go down to Mexico, or to South America."

I didn't say anything.

She rolled lazily onto her back, cupped her hands behind her neck, and gazed up at the sky. "Couldn't we stay here for two days, Martin?"

"Hardly."

"You'd rather be back on the ship than here, wouldn't you?"

"I would."

She turned her head and smiled. "Darling, it's not easy to keep a one-sided conversation going. Really, it isn't. You must do better than one or two words."

"I'm not a talker, Joyce. You know that."

"As a matter of fact, I didn't." She came up on her elbow. "Oh, what a cute child!"

The kid was far from cute as he came waddling along the path. He was about five, all belly, cheeks, and a running nose. Joyce called to him. He stopped and gave her a suspicious look.

"Give me a dollar, Martin."

I gave her the coin. She held it out to the kid, smiling and assuring him they were friends.

As I watched her coaxing the kid over, it was hard for me to realize this same woman had coldly plotted her husband's murder. With her voice gentle, and the late sunlight softening the lines in her face, everything that had happened aboard the Trader suddenly began to seem unreal, as if it had taken place in a dream.

Only for a moment did it seem that way; the kid made a grab for the coin, and when Joyce flinched from the touch of his grubby fingers the illusion that she was anything but a first-class bitch was broken. She was trying hard to act like a human being, but it was only acting. And lousy acting. It reminded me I was sitting here with her because she had willed it, that we were married because she felt more comfortable that way. It reminded me she not only murdered a man but got worked up over the act.

"Let's go, Joyce."

We walked back to the inn in silence. She gave me a sly look at the door.

"Give me ten minutes, Martin."

I gave her fifteen, walking around outside while the Chinese woman and two of her kids stood giggling at me from the doorway.

"A bottle of wine and flowers. Wasn't that sweet of them, Martin? They must have known we were just married."

I sat in the only chair in the room, smoking, watching her fuss with some blue and yellow flowers in a cracked vase. A four-poster bed, one rickety table with an enamel basin, and the chair I was sitting on were the total furnishings. The two windows were covered with something that looked like burlap and a bamboo mat covered the floor. Another basin sat under the bed.

One small candle conveniently kept down the glare of blood-red wallpaper.

"Shall we have the wine now, Martin?"

"O.K."

She filled the two glasses that had been provided and handed me one. "Do you like my pajamas?"

I said I did. They were the Japanese type, white silk edged with black, the wide trouser cuffs stopping short of her calves. Her dark hair was down and it fanned across her shoulders, giving her thin face a small-girl look.

She sipped the wine, puckering her lips. "Hmmm, bitter."

She wandered slowly around the room, making a pretense of studying the cracks in the wallpaper, occasionally giving me a look from the corner of her eye. The pajama bottoms kept flapping around her legs, and for some reason this annoyed me.

"It's not much of a place, is it, Martin?"

"Not much."

"You'd think they would at least put real curtains up. It would make quite a change, I think."

I agreed it would make a change.

She smiled. "Today is not one of your talking days, I see."

I agreed again.

She stopped by the small table, bent over, and blew the candle out. No light came through the windows. She made no sound in the darkness, just the soft rustle of silk. Then quiet. She waited.

I struck a match and got up.

"Martin, *please....*"

I went over and touched it to the candle. I turned and looked at her.

She was smiling a protest, using her hands to cover her nakedness. The tender-bride routine.

"Darling, *must* we have the light?"

"Put your hands down, Joyce. Let me look at you."

She slowly put them down, smiling demurely. A hungry look crept into her eyes as she took a step toward me, her arms half extended.

I meant at that moment to turn and walk out. I had planned it that way. Just a simple rebuff to show her how things stood, how they would always stand.

But I didn't walk out. I stood there, letting my eyes travel over her full breasts and her thighs; and my disgust mounted. I remembered the way she acted after she thought she had committed murder. It wasn't enough to just walk out. I wanted to hurt her. Not physically, but in a way only a woman can be hurt.

"Darling...." She extended her arms fully, her eyes now heavy-lidded, her lips still smiling.

"Joyce, one thing always bothered me at sea: the sight of a half-sick rat crawling down a gutter. That's one sight I could never stand." My eyes kept wandering over her. "That's the way I feel now, Joyce. Just looking at you makes me want to throw up."

Her smile froze. The blood began draining from her face.

I turned to go and she leaped after me. Her nails raked the side of my face, carrying skin away. I caught her arms.

She kicked and struggled to get free.

"You bastard! You dirty, rotten, egotistical bastard!"

She freed one hand and clawed me again. I twisted her around, remembering then what I had promised myself to do.

The kick against her shapely rump sent her flying against the four-poster. She bounced off that and went sprawling on her back to the floor. She lay there stunned for a moment, her eyes closed.

"I think you missed your calling, Joyce. That position looks too natural."

Her eyes opened, filling with pain and hate. Savagely she bared her teeth.

"You'll pay! God help me, you'll pay!"

"Your crime is heavier, Joyce, so better think twice before doing anything. You can't hurt me now, with half the Trader mine. When we reach the States I'm putting you ashore. You'll get the monthly accounting that a partner is entitled to, but you're not living aboard any more. You see, I'm not only half owner, but still captain—and I've decided it's impractical to carry passengers any longer."

I reached Shanghai at dawn, managed to get dead drunk at noon and into one hell of a scrap with a Portuguese who stopped pushing my face in out of sheer pity. I woke up in my cabin, Garrett taking my clothes off.

"Lad, you've had a time."

Something kept beating me on the top of my head. I put my hand up and felt bandages. My nose was clogged with blood. I couldn't open one eye. Across my cheekbone were some stitches.

"Put something cold on my head, will you, Pappy?"

He got a towel, wet it, and put it over my forehead. I closed the one eye and heard eight bells being struck off, each one sending a sliver of pain through my head.

"What's the hour, Pappy?"

"Midnight."

I sensed then the feel of open water under the vessel. "Under way, eh? She aboard?"

"She's aboard. Came in the sampan they put you in."

My head began pounding again. "That boy did a job, all right. Who did the patching up?"

"If you mean the bandages, a doctor ashore did that. The stitching on your cheek, I did."

"What the hell was wrong with the doc's doing it?"

"Maybe there was nothing to stitch at the time."

I opened my eye. Garrett was putting on his coat and hat. He went over to the door.

"Pappy, was I alone in that sampan with Mrs. Sloan?"

He turned with his hand on the door. His faded eyes were grim.

"You were alone with her coming back to the ship."

After Garrett left I fell asleep trying to figure out what Joyce had found in the sampan to use on my face.

Chapter Fourteen

Garrett nodded to me and kept working with the dividers. "Still dropping fast, lad. We're in for the show, all right."

"What's the latest on it?"

"North of Okinawa and circling. It's edging south with gale force. We're directly in the path." He put a blunt finger on the chart. "By tomorrow night we'll be moving across the Roamers, and I've been thinking we might do well to move south of the light, well clear of the shoal legs. Chances are we'll be running blind and doing a lot of guesswork."

I leaned on the chart board, resting my aching head in my hands. Even with twenty-four hours' sleep I felt I was coming apart at the seams. I had a touch of fever, too, which didn't help matters any.

"Whatever you say, Pappy. Better go below and rig some deck lines. I'll take over for a while up here."

He reached for his raincoat. "Gerlack's improving. At least, his fever is dropping some. The rash is all over his face, so there's no doubt that he had the measles."

"No doubt."

"You don't look too bad, considering the banging around you took."

"That's one advantage in having a pan like mine; it always looks beat up. Better check the boom cradles while you're at it, Pappy. Might be a good idea to double the strapping."

I went outside and walked around the weather deck, the spray and sharp wind cooling my face. It wasn't the brightest thing to do for a fever, but I wanted to clear my head of a peculiar feeling of being crowded. It was hard to explain, but since I had wakened I had a feeling that something was out of place, in the sounds about me, or in the feel of the ship.

I stood out on the dark wing, listening to the steady throb of the Diesels, the quick pound of the sloping seas against the sides, the moan of the night wind, all the familiar sounds you take for granted and hardly notice when a ship is bucking heavy seas. Something was wrong, but what?

I worried it along a few minutes, gave it up as a bad job, and went into the wheelhouse. Walters was behind the wheel.

"Rough night, eh, Cap? Mr. Garrett was saying it would get worse if anything."

I didn't feel like talking. I poured some coffee from the thermos. The cup was halfway to my mouth when it struck me again, the false note somewhere. I stood motionless with the cup, listening hard, trying to narrow it down. It was a faint sound, rhythmic but faint, as elusive to place as a pulse beat. Like someone tapping against metal or wood. Like someone on a deck below poking metal a stick at the deck.

Like the sound Sloan used to make when he limped across the deck on his cane.

Walters was staring at me. "Cap, you sick?" He left the wheel and came over.

"Get back on that wheel!"

"Maybe if you sat down, Cap—"

"Take your hands off me and do as you're told!"

He went back to the wheel and kept his square jaw pointed at the binnacle.

I gulped down the coffee. My hand trembled so much I could hardly hold the cup. In the condition I was in it had got me for a moment, that tapping sound. It was probably in the engine room, the sound being transmitted up through the plates. It happens.

"Walters."

He was sore and didn't turn around. "Yes, sir?"

"Hear anything out of place?"

"No, sir. Don't think so."

"You have to listen a while to hear it."

He listened. "No, sir. What should I hear?"

Fine, Lewandowski. Great. Next you'll be hearing him whisper.

Ferguson was half dozing on the stool, a magazine lying in his lap. He saw me and opened the magazine. He never had much to say except when it concerned the ship, which was O.K. with me.

I walked around the floor plates a few minutes and came back and stood by the main engines, listening. "Little noisy, aren't they, Ferguson? The engines?"

He kept on reading. "I hadn't noticed."

"Sure nothing is loose?"

"I don't run loose engines."

I was standing directly beside the main engine. Even while he was speaking I heard it, no louder, no softer than anywhere else, the same monotonous tapping, as if Sloan were limping along a lower deck. It was either the engines or in my head.

"I think I hear a tap, Ferguson. It may be coming from that engine."

He looked up in disgust. "Like I said, there's nothing—" He stopped and looked surprised. "You don't mean that crank-pin knock? Some hearing you have if that's been bothering you."

"How long has it been loose?"

He began filling his pipe, deliberately taking his time answering. "Wouldn't call it exactly loose. Needs keying a bit."

"How long has it been that way?"

"Few hours." He stopped filling his pipe. "Maybe you want me to shut down and fix it?"

It was the way he said it, heavy with sarcasm. I didn't want the engines shut down. I didn't give a damn about the pin knocking. I had just been curious how long it had been that way. He'd picked one lousy time to needle me.

"You guessed it, Ferguson. Hop to it!"

"You can't be serious!" His mustache twitched.

"I'm serious."

"That would be a dismantling job."

I went over to the engine telegraph and swung it to "Stop." "Notify the bridge you'll be laying to until repairs are made. Hustle out your men and get on with it."

He hopped off the stool, steaming. "It's ridiculous! It'll take a day."

"Wrong. It'll take a half day. To be more specific, at noon, if we're not under way again, start congratulating your first assistant on his promotion to chief."

I bumped into Garrett in the dark of the well deck, along the railing. He grabbed my arm. "Lad, you can't be serious about laying to and lifting that engine?"

"It'll only take a few hours." I was beginning to feel a little foolish about the whole matter, but I didn't know how to back down. I hadn't been thinking clearly and knew it. Maybe it was the fever, or maybe the load I'd taken on in Shanghai.

"Martin, I've a question. If you don't answer it, that's all right." The expression in his eyes was masked by the darkness. He drew a breath. "Did you have anything to do with Sloan's dying?"

The question rocked me. I forgot my head. "How the devil could I have anything to do with his dying? He just died, that's all. Maybe sickness, maybe old age. I don't know."

"You didn't answer me, Martin. If you can't—"

"Of course I can answer. It's no! Listen, if you have any suspicions he died otherwise, just let me know and we'll go into it." I waited.

He shook his head. "No, lad. I haven't. It's just

that too many things are happening that shouldn't be. Too many things that don't make sense. Like that woman, with you in the sampan. Why did she want to hurt you like that?"

"Who said she did? Maybe whoever put me in the sampan wasn't too gentle. Maybe I hit my face on the thwart."

"Martin, I spoke to that sampan coolie after Mrs. Sloan went into her cabin. I didn't catch much of what he said, but I got the idea he peeked through the canopy flaps on the way out and saw her using the heel of her shoe on your face."

"That's nonsense, Pappy. You probably misunderstood him. What else is going on that's bothering you?"

He shrugged. "Maybe it's your drinking so much. Maybe it's blowing your top with Ferguson over minor engine trouble. Little things, Martin, that aren't like you. Even the crew has noticed your change since—since Sloan's death."

I had to know. "Mean they think I had something to do with his dying?"

"Hell, no. Nothing like that."

"Just *you* thought so, eh?"

He looked ashamed. "Lad, I did and I didn't. I knew—I guess everybody did—that Sloan's wife had taken to you and ... well, I couldn't help but speculate."

"Pappy, I've committed lots of sins in my time, but murdering old men is not one of them. I don't even like the subject, so suppose we drop it."

"All right, Martin. Sorry I brought it up. I think you might drink a little less, though. It's starting talk in the fo'c'sle. And this tiff with Ferguson—"

"He rubbed me the wrong way, that's all. He was giving me the needle and I socked it right back at him. O.K., Pappy, I'm wrong. Go below and tell him to forget the job."

Whether a skipper is liked or disliked, he is on a pedestal and in the limelight at all times. The slightest thing he publicly does aboard the ship is open to close scrutiny and sometimes criticism. And should any of his actions border on the irrational, it becomes at once a subject for discussion by the hands. Aboard a ship at sea this is never good. Once a seaman's inbred respect for the bridge is lost, contempt follows, and a feeling of insecurity arises. A good skipper knows this and is constantly on his toes to guard his prestige. Slip down from that pedestal and you leave yourself open for trouble.

I was reminded of my slip the following afternoon on the boat deck when I was making a last check on the gear, seeing that everything was well secured for the heavy weather. Joyce came out of her cabin and walked my way. It was the first time I'd seen her since leaving port. Her face had a determined look.

"I heard about last night. I think you'd better stay away from the bottle."

The last drink I had was in Shanghai, and the way I felt at the moment it would be the last for some time. "What the devil are you talking about?"

"I'm talking about your drinking, and your imagining things. Oh, I heard all about it, how you were going around trying to trace down a tapping noise."

"That wasn't imagination. That noise was in the engines."

"Was it, now? And what did you think before you located it?"

"I didn't think anything. I—"

"As soon as I heard the engineers discussing it, how slight the sound was, I knew what was bothering you. You were hearing Ezra's cane, weren't you?"

"Joyce—"

"If you start imagining things—"

"Listen, get it into your skull I didn't imagine it!"

"Well, you soon will if you keep uncorking bottles. Watch out that Ezra doesn't hop up out of the next one waving his cane at you!"

I was tempted to slug her but didn't. I saw the play to get my goat; she wanted to get back at me in some way but didn't know how.

I turned my back and moved over to the starboard lifeboat. She followed me.

"Don't you think we have things to talk about?"

"We have nothing to talk about."

"We *are* married, you know."

I kept my back to her and inspected the lifeboat lashings. "Only in name. You stay on your side of the fence and everything will be fine. You can do anything you please, go anywhere you please. I don't give a damn what you do as long as you stay away from me. Far away."

She was silent a moment. I started adjusting a lashing, wishing she'd beat it.

"Martin, I'm willing to forget the past. All of it."

"I'm not."

"You still think the same of me, all the things you said?"

"I never say anything I don't mean. I want no part of you."

She was silent again. Then she was breathing close to my ear, almost hissing the words.

"All right. I'm finished with you, you dirty Polack! That's what you are: a dirty Polack with a loud mouth. I've taken enough. Now it's your turn. Let's see if your skin is so tough. You've hurt me and now it's your turn. Before this trip is out we'll see who's the stronger,"

After she left I went down to my room, swallowed some aspirins, and tried to get some sleep.

She had sworn to get even, and I knew her well enough to believe that in one way or another she'd attempt to do just that. But what form would it take?

I doubted she'd try anything violent. I had an idea she'd try taking me down a peg—if she could. How would she go about it?

It was enough to keep me awake.

Chapter Fifteen

The wheelhouse was like a tomb. Garrett stood by the window, grimly watching the evening sky darken with the approaching storm. Phelps kept fussing over the chart with a straight rule and dividers, as if he could in some way change things. Cutrone was behind the wheel, his legs spread wide, his hairy hands gripping the wheel, as if it were going to be a personal battle between him and the elements.

We were in for it, all right. It was in the air you tried to breathe. You had to open your mouth to get enough of it, and when you did it tasted dry and sulphury.

Garrett moved away from the window and came over to where I was leaning on the telegraph. I had to lean on something.

"You look bushed, Martin. Why don't you go below and catch some sleep?"

"Later, maybe."

He tilted his head at the window.

"Think it'd pay to run from this? That front is two hundred miles, but we could try to circle. Once we get in we'll have to slow to bare steerage and that'll mean a day or two of pounding. Maybe more if it shifts."

"That's the gimmick, Pappy. If we try to circle she may shift again too and be right with us. We'll have to stick it out."

The coming storm was only one of my worries. An hour before I had passed Joyce in the passageway and I'd got a look I couldn't figure. She hadn't said a word, but she looked so much like the cat that swallowed the mouse I knew something was cooking. But what?

A blast of wind suddenly sent the freighter careening.

Cutrone swore and brought the wheel over. Ahead of us, a few miles distant, the choppy sea was disappearing under an approaching dark mass that hung billowing from the swollen sky like a huge wind-blown veil.

"Pappy, go down and tell all hands to stay below except when necessary to relieve the watch. Phelps, you check those life lines again. See that they're well secured. And both of you stay below. No sense wandering around unless you have to."

Ten minutes after they left the storm enveloped us and the freighter began moving into a dark world of lashing rains and running seas. I rang down for one-third speed as she plunged into deepening troughs, smashing headlong against dark curling walls that sent spray flying over the bridge house. Another ten minutes and I called for bare steerage; a screaming wind had whipped in from the southeast and we were staggering in hammering seas, moving blindly through torrential rains.

The Trader was now shuddering under the impacts, hesitating longer moments before she groggily rose, coming up like a punch-drunk fighter, trembling and shaking, the foaming waters cascading from the foredecks.

Cutrone kept crossing himself, his eyes on the fury outside.

"Keep checking that mark, Cutrone. Save those prayers for later. You may need them."

"Sure, Cap."

An hour passed without any letup in the wind or rain. Garrett came up to report that the entire starboard railing had been carried away, including the gangway that had been lashed to it. All canvas was shredded, and the galley was a shambles; Silva had neglected to secure the utilities.

"All right, Pappy. We can't stop damage. There'll be plenty before this is over. When you see Silva, take a piece out of him for not being on the ball."

He turned to go, then stopped. "Mrs. Sloan wants you to bring in the account books when you go off."

"At midnight?"

He shrugged. "Said if she's asleep just leave them on the table outside. Seems she wants something to do in case she wakes up, to keep her from getting seasick or something."

"O.K., Pappy."

Something smelled fishy. What the devil did she want now?

At eleven o'clock the wind abated somewhat and the heavy rain stopped completely. But the seas continued to run high, keeping the decks constantly awash. When Phelps came up to relieve me he brought the latest report on the storm. I plotted it out and saw that the worst was still ahead of us.

Phelps looked nervous. "I suppose we couldn't turn back to port or anything like that?"

"You bet we couldn't. If we turned back every time we hit heavy weather we'd be out of business fast. We're in good shape, don't worry about it."

I went below and got out the two ledgers Joyce wanted. They contained all transactions to date. As a precaution I took a pistol from my trunk, loaded it, and dropped it in my pocket. It seemed inconceivable I'd have any use for it just then, but it was a comfortable feeling just having it with me.

No lights were on in the cabin when I approached the door. I opened it gently and stepped inside. Immediately I stood stock-still, unable to see in the darkness but all other senses overwhelmed by the muffled cries of pleasure coming from the inner room, the steaming passion you could almost feel.

It took me only a moment to get over the shock, and another moment to grasp the fact that Joyce had planned it this way. This was her so-called revenge, her seeing how thick my skin was. Maybe she thought it would hurt, now that she was my wife; or maybe she meant to show me exactly what I had meant to her in the past. But whatever effect she meant it to have on me, I felt only disgust, and then curiosity—curiosity as to her partner.

I fumbled for the light switch at the cabin door, found it.

The overhead light flashed on, cutting past the open doorway into the bedroom. I stared at the scene. I wanted to laugh but didn't. I settled for a grin at the farcical sight of Silva, his mouth open as he got up. I kept grinning, and Joyce's wooden smile disappeared.

"You'll have to try again, Joyce."

I walked out chuckling over the sheer frustration of her play. The hunched figure of Garrett came across the rolling deck, a cloud of spray sweeping after him.

"Just came in, lad." He pulled a slip of paper from beneath his raincoat. "Jap tanker breaking up. About forty miles east. If we go we'll have our tail spanked all the way."

The distress call was for the Kora Maru. She was in bad shape, her deck plates cracking and all lifeboats smashed. "Anyone closer?"

"Nobody else answered."

"O.K., Pappy, we'll take it. Tell them we're proceeding full speed. I'll check below and be right up to keep you company."

I forgot about Joyce and Silva. Northwest of us was a doomed vessel, helpless men whose lives depended on the Trader's ability to make time in the storm. When you follow the sea the drama of this grips you. Nothing else is on your mind. Nothing counts except the race that will determine whether men will live or die.

Ferguson was hopping around below when I hit the floor plates. He came over sputtering and waving his arms.

"We can't do it, Captain! We can't. Just listen to it!"

I didn't have to listen. The wind was at our stern, and each time the counter rose over the rushing seas, the screw spun wildly, shaking everything so violently you expected it to tear loose.

"What are you running, Ferguson?"

"Fifty, and I can't be responsible—"

"You won't have any responsibility left if you don't get it to sixty. Did Garrett order full speed?"

"Yes, but—"

"Boost it. Pronto!"

I hung around for a while watching Ferguson and the assistant sweat over the engines. I wanted to get the feel of how much she'd take; it wouldn't do that Jap one bit of good if we broke down.

But except for a leak that developed in the stern tube gland, the Trader took the punishment. Ferguson kept mumbling about his spring bearings aft but shut up when I asked if he'd be worrying so much about spring bearings on the Jap if she was coming to a floundering Trader.

I went topside and worked my way forward on the hand lines, ten feet at a time. Each time the freighter rolled, waist-high seas came spilling across the sloping deck, scouring the steel to slippery glasslike footing. You didn't move at these times, you held on and waited for the creamy waters to run off. Occasionally, lightning would cleave the darkness and you caught sight of the rushing gray forms alongside, the foam-flecked crests. It reminded you of the fury about you, waiting for your guard to be lowered ... like that Jap vessel's.

At the head of the companionway I met Silva

coming from the cabin. He looked straight at me as he went by, not at all worried by anything I might be thinking. But then, why should he be worried? When you're like that with the owner, what's a mere captain?

I stayed on the bridge with Garrett, both of us training glasses forward, waiting for the momentary lightning flashes to light the horizon ahead. At three o'clock we spotted the tanker—and without glasses. An orange haze suddenly appeared in the distance off our bow.

Garrett softly swore. "Fire aboard, lad. With smashed lifeboats they're between the devil and the deep for sure."

We changed course, heading directly for the orange glow under emergency speed. I could almost feel the panic that must be aboard, the terrorized men scanning the seas for the Trader. Twice I went over to the engine-room phone and cursed more speed from Ferguson. The entire vessel was now shaking so violently she wouldn't have a tight bolt in another hour, but that was all we needed. One hour.

"Pappy, round up your strongest men. There's brandy in my room. Let them polish off a bottle, then ready a boat."

We came up on the burning tanker, cutting to leeward of it. The vessel itself was a mess. She was down at the bow, the bridge house a mass of wreckage dragging over the side, twisting in the reddened seas. Both masts were gone and there was a queer rake to her sides that told of a warped hull. Her fire was forward, a fifty-foot circular shaft of flame roaring up from a manhole and looking much like a giant blowtorch in the night. It was apparent the fire had been caused by the manhole cover rupturing or twisting off, setting off the gasoline beneath. Only a miracle had staved off an explosion.

On the tanker's stern huddled perhaps a dozen

figures, their pale faces turned to us as we began to circle and pump oil over the side to smooth the seas. There was danger that the oil would be set afire but to lower a boat in the wild seas between the two ships would have been suicide.

With the wheel hard over and at top speed the Trader circled twice, spilling her heavy fuel oil. Phelps came up on the bridge and almost bowled me over by saying he'd like to head the lifeboat. Just shows you never know a man.

"I'm taking it, Phelps. Thanks anyway. Listen, you get hold of Silva and see if he can get some hot coffee going. They'll—"

The rending sound of buckling steel cut me off. As if it were nothing more than a toy, the tanker had suddenly split in two, a ragged break at midships with thousands of gallons of gasoline flowing from the broken tanks. For an instant you could see the gas mixing with the oil, the horrified expressions of the doomed men huddled on the stern section. For an instant you saw this picture, then came the walls of flame sweeping out from the severed ship; no explosion, just sheets of flame leaping in all directions as ruptured tanks spewed gasoline onto the waters.

Half sick from the knowledge that we had failed, that we were to watch men die, I shouted the order to back down, away from the spreading sea of fire. There was nothing we could do. Not one damn thing. Except watch.

Garrett came over and stood beside me. "Poor devils." He kept repeating it over and over.

We stood and watched, and waited. We couldn't leave until the huddled figures on the tanker's stern were gone. We had to stay, and hope for a chance to move in and save them. Fat chance.

The forward half of the tanker settled quickly, the flaming sea spitting vapor and debris as she vanished from sight. Only the after section remained, the stern tilting higher as she upended and slowly filled with water. I watched one of the figures on the stern climb up on the railing, pausing momentarily as if taking a deep breath. He dove off, down into the black smoking flames.

What he was attempting to do was hopeless. An unbroken circle of fire surrounded the broken ship for two hundred yards. He came up after maybe thirty yards. His screams came clearly to the Trader. They lasted perhaps ten seconds. None of the others tried it. They wanted to live a bit longer. They did. About two minutes longer. With a belch and a hissing roar the stern slid slowly out of sight, the writhing flames, pulled in by suction, covering the spot where she disappeared. Only a few heads bobbed to the surface, threshing their arms in the flames, screaming, their faces contorted with agony.

It was a scene out of hell itself.

Garrett nudged me. "Look at her, lad. No, topside."

I turned and saw Joyce watching the flaming waters from the flying bridge, her loose black hair blowing wildly behind her. Although her white face was without expression, her green eyes held a peculiar hungry glow, as if they were attempting to devour the misery before it ended.

"Martin, that's the way she looked when Sandora's body was taken from the fender. Is it the reflection of the fire or is that woman enjoying this?"

She was enjoying it, all right. But nothing about Joyce surprised me anymore.

"It's just the fire, Pappy."

Joyce turned slightly, saw me staring up. Her eyes suddenly grew cold and brittle. They told me more plainly than words that she'd be playing no more games, that her next move against me would be for keeps if she got the opportunity.

I walked off the bridge, toying with the thought of

putting Silva under lock and key until we reached Frisco. Joyce, alone, I could keep one step ahead of, but with Silva as a helpmate she wouldn't have too hard a job getting rid of me. I saw a dozen ways they could do a slick job.

For the first time since I'd shipped to sea I snapped the inside lock on my door before hitting the bunk.

Chapter Sixteen

We got under way again at dawn, heading eastward into gusty winds of gale force that drove racing scud before it. At noon the wind shifted, coming out of the south, and with it came a freak movement of the storm. We had figured to pass out of its perimeter that very day, leaving it behind, but instead we found it sweeping behind us in a widening arc, its intensity increasing.

Warnings about hurricanes of destructive force were being flashed all over the northwest Pacific, and Garrett and I went into a huddle on what course to follow. For an hour we plotted and replotted the storm. The feeling of tension among the crew had increased after they learned of the hurricane report and, to them, our decision should be a simple one to make: Head for the nearest port or continue eastward to get away from the storm area. But it wasn't that simple. We had no desire to head back for the China coast and be caught near the shoreline in broaching seas. And continuing eastward might mean running with the storm if it should veer out to sea, taking the brunt of the punishment for the entire duration of the blow.

I finally decided to head south and ride straight into it, taking the calculated risk of eight or nine hours of pounding. The time element is always the factor in any storm. A ship can get pounded just so long and then, like a human, will go limp, the fight sapped out of her. Whether a vessel is big or small, that time factor remains the same. It can take just so much.

"I hope you're right, lad." Garrett was plainly worried.

"Look, Pappy, I may be stubborn at times, but I'm no fool. You've been riding this stuff for thirty years. Say we do better going east or west, and we'll go."

José, the little Cuban, turned from the wheel and looked over at us. "Maybe it's better we go to Japanese port."

"You keep your eye on that mark! What is it, Pappy?"

Garrett finally shrugged. "A tossup, I'd say. If we can move in and get out by morning we'll be ahead of the game, all right. The question is: Will the storm shift again?"

It was a big question.

By dusk we were in the teeth of it, a wailing wind overhead and green water over our bow. Through the bridge windows nothing was visible, the wind-driven spray obscuring everything ahead of us, the constant roar of sea and wind drowning all other sounds. Occasionally a glimpse was had of the fo'c'sle, the boiling seas racing across it.

By midnight Garrett's question was answered. The wind shifted to our port quarter. Garrett and I looked at one another. There was nothing to do but sit tight and wait it out.

Phelps was the first to hear the rumor that the Trader was to be scuttled for insurance. In bad weather silly rumors are always being started, and I told him to forget it. But by morning he hadn't forgotten it, and neither had I. The rumor had not petered out as rumors usually do, but spread from the fo'c'sle aft. What made it worse was the loss of one lifeboat during the night. Then somebody got the bright idea of wearing a life jacket at all times and the idea caught on. All hands appeared with the jackets.

Garrett gave me the full dope on the rumor: Now that Sloan was dead, the Trader's business was expected to fall off and she was worth more on the bottom; I had ordered her course directly into the storm so I would have an excuse to abandon her.

"They should know better, Pappy. What the hell would I have to gain from abandoning ship?"

"The talk is you're in for a piece of the insurance if it comes off. Don't ask me who dreamed up a thing like that. It started somewhere and each man is adding his bit."

"Any idea of who's doing the most talking?"

He shrugged. "Silva's been trying to get together a delegation to insist we head back for Shanghai. That's bad. Someone could get hurt if the crew started ganging together on this."

It fell into place then. Joyce had rolled a snowball and handed it to Silva. Why I hadn't seen it instantly I didn't know. Someone could get hurt, all right, and it could damn well be me. An argument with the hands, a little milling around after seeing that the officers were occupied with something else, and Captain Lewandowski could wind up with his brains spilled in the fo'c'sle. Maybe Silva would see to that. And mum would be the word if it did happen. Those babies in the fo'c'sle would clam right up on a job like that.

Too bad the skipper fell and hit his head. Tough, but it happens.

"Martin, this can get out of hand. Fast."

"O.K., Pappy, I'll handle it. I can play a cute game too. I want every hand in the fo'c'sle to assemble in my room within ten minutes. Leave Silva out of it. I might be tempted to squeeze that fat neck until the juice runs if he shows his face."

They filed into the room, the sea water running from their oilskins, their expressions a little sullen. I waited until the door was closed and they were lined up looking at me. Then I waited some more, staring at each one until the sullenness was replaced by some uneasiness.

I pulled a paper from my drawer, placed it on the desk, and appeared to study it. Occasionally I glanced up at a man and frowned, as if some particular item on the paper had displeased me.

Finally I pushed the paper aside.

"Let's get down to cases. Is there any man here so stupid as to believe he can so much as sneeze on this ship without my hearing about it—when I want to hear?"

They didn't get it. A few glanced at one another. Cutrone scratched his head. José scratched his. Blake, a slick-haired lady's man, fingered his pencil mustache.

"I have here a few items about each of you, things you have done and said on this trip. Someone I have a lot of faith in is willing to swear the list is correct should the occasion arise. That occasion, of course, would be an inquiry over any trouble aboard."

It began to penetrate then. One by one they worriedly glanced down at the paper. A brown nose in the fo'c'sle is not too unusual a thing. Aboard the Trader I hadn't found anyone carrying tales to the bridge, but that didn't stop me from giving the impression that I had. And there wasn't a man in the room who hadn't been griping about the pay cuts or the heavier work they'd been doing. Those gripes meant nothing, sure; I knew it as well as they did.

But I saw the struggle in their faces as they tried to recall what loose talk they'd done in the past.

I lit a cigarette and leaned back in the chair, watching them fidget, shift their feet. With the chances of a pigeon being in the fo'c'sle, each man would talk a damn sight less in the future, and be careful of his actions. A crew of men can be persuaded pretty easily into rough action under trying conditions; when guilt is divided a dozen ways, it doesn't seem like guilt at all. But be in a position to pin it on one man; make each realize *his* speech and actions are personal things; in short, let it be known someone in the fo'c'sle has a direct wire to the cabin, and you don't get trouble born of idle rumors.

I glanced at the paper again, then looked up at Cutrone. He'd always been a loud mouth. The ship's toughie.

"You, Cutrone. I don't like the idea of suggesting it would be nice if someone pushed me over the side during this blow."

Cutrone's head came up. The muscles jumped in his swarthy face. "Geeze, Cap! I look crazy? Why I say that?"

"Well, did you?"

He folded his arms across his chest and glared at me. "No!"

"Never made any threats against me? Think it over carefully."

He stopped glaring and his eyes shifted worriedly to the other men. Damn right he'd made threats. Chances were he couldn't remember a single one, but he'd said plenty.

"We'll come back to you later." I tilted my head to Widemeyer. He was known for his appetite, and I'd seen him a number of times hanging out in the galley, giving Silva a hand with the dishes for a handout.

"Widemeyer, you're been in huddles with Silva too damn much. I understand you recently had a little discussion with him about me."

He wet his lips. "Gee, Skipper, I ain't never said nothin' against you. I mean, I ain't never meant nothin'. I mean it wasn't nothin'."

I saw I struck oil here. "I've heard from this

certain source that you mentioned to Silva that the ship would be better off without me, that if something happened to me—"

His eyes popped. "No, Skipper! Not *that* way! Sure, I said somethin' to him, but you know the stuff I'd say. Kiddin' stuff. It don't mean nothin'!"

"Just what did you tell Silva that meant nothing?"

"Nothin', Cap, so help—"

"Widemeyer, I'm not looking for a fall guy. I just want the truth. I'll decide whether you were talking from the side of your mouth."

"Sure, Cap, just gabbin'. Like you said, from the side of my mouth. It meant nothin'."

"What was it you said?"

He looked to the men for support. They were curious too.

"It was nothin', Cap. Just ... Well, you know how Silva used to go around stickin' the point of the knife at a guy. When he did it to me, I'd tell him—" He pulled out a dirty handkerchief, began wiping his face.

"Yes?" I had an idea what was coming.

He took a deep breath. "To shove it at the skipper instead!"

No one even snickered.

"What did he say?"

"He said— Hell, Skipper, I just don't remember! Maybe like he'd try it. But, he wasn't serious. He'd just start grinning. You know how he is."

I nodded, picked up the paper, gave it a final glance, then put it back in the drawer. I made a show of carefully locking the drawer, almost able to feel their eyes on me.

"I understand there's been some anxiety since we lost the Number Two boat. In case anyone has doubts about who gets in the remaining boat, if such a necessity arises, it's the lowest-ranking men on the ship. Mrs. Sloan first, of course, but the hands after that. Officers will use the raft aft."

I looked up at them, as much as to say I'd be a damn fool to sink a ship without a good sound boat waiting for me.

"That's about all. Just one thing more: If anyone feels insecure on deck, not strong enough to manage the hand lines, you have my permission to stay below, relieved of watches until the storm blows over; you can pay back later whoever picks up for you. The sight of big strapping seamen wearing life jackets on deck is making Mrs. Sloan nervous. I don't blame her much, do you?"

I gave them a man-to-man smile then, and began getting sheepish ones back.

When they filed out they were looking for all the world like a bunch of school kids leaving the teacher's office.

I felt pretty satisfied with myself. This one had been my round. If Joyce wanted to collect my scalp, she'd have to be a bit more clever about it.

Or maybe less clever.

I thought that one out. With the decks constantly awash, it was an easy thing to get rid of a man, especially the skipper. He's the one guy who is all over the ship in a storm. In heavy weather, day and night, he's the one guy who will pass any given spot at least once, and if you waited you would be able to meet him wherever you chose to.

If Joyce wanted to get rid of me bad enough, now would be the time to do it, while the storm continued to rage. A knife thrust and a push by Silva would do the trick. He wouldn't even have to push. The seas would take care of that.

It gave me something to think about.

I was just dozing off when a new sound joined the shrill wind outside. It started as a distant growl, muffled by wind and wave. Half asleep, I heard the growl rise steadily like an oncoming express train.

And suddenly I was wide awake with memory flashing pictures of the freak combers that plague the China coast, the speeding wall of water, the yawning chasm falling away before it.

I was off the bunk the instant the Trader twisted sideways and went into a sickening plunge. The room tilted crazily. I went floundering, trying to maintain balance. The comber struck then, broadside, halting the vessel's plunge and wrenching it back the other way. My hands had been reaching for the wall, and it was as if somebody had suddenly flung the steel bulkhead at my head.

I remembered the jolting pain, the orange-streaked darkness. I remembered trying to reach into the darkness for something to hold onto.

I remembered falling a long, long way....

"Stop fighting me, lad! Drink this. Careful now...."

I gagged on the water and pushed the glass away. I tried to get up. Garrett, sitting on the edge of my bunk, forced me back. He was gaunt and hollow-eyed, one side of his face streaked with oil. He kept a big hand on my chest, holding me down.

"I had a time carrying you to this bunk, so you stay put a while."

Something seemed to be sitting on my head. I put my hand up and felt a sticky egg-shaped swelling.

Garrett nodded and got to his feet. "You've really got a head now. If it feels the way it looks, you feel plenty bad."

I swung my feet onto the floor, squeezing my eyes against the splitting pain.

"How long have I been out?"

"Maybe thirty minutes. Listen, lad, stay in your bunk. The shoring is being completed."

"*Shoring!*" I grabbed my head to keep it from coming apart. "How much damage, Pappy?"

"Well, three buckled plates in the engine room is the only serious damage. Ferguson's got it pretty much under control. Listen, lad...."

I pushed Garrett aside and went staggering outside.

It was dawn, the sky overhead ragged and hurrying northward. On each side of the wallowing deck billowing seas raced aft, as if trying to catch up with the surface spray blown along by the wind. Our decks were a shambles. Both booms on the well deck had been wrenched from their mooring cradles and were lying across the Number Two hold. Our remaining lifeboat was a twisted piece of metal wedged between the cargo winches. Splintered wood, wire, and an assortment of galley utensils were strewn everywhere.

When I reached the engine room Ferguson and his gang were sloshing around in a foot of oily water. Mattresses had been jammed against the buckled plates with supporting timbers, and the hands were pouring cement into the crude cofferdam they'd erected. The plates involved were just below the water line, making the work difficult, but it was a pretty effective job of shoring.

I felt like sitting down somewhere and nursing my head, but I kept looking at the shoring, gauging the small amount of water seeping through, the relatively small amount covering the floor plates. Something was wrong; at least, it felt that way in the ponderous roll of the vessel.

Ferguson stopped to wipe his perspiring face. His long mustache was gray-black with cement and oil.

"We'll be dry in an hour or so if the plates don't open on us. But we can't take another like that, I can tell you that."

I kept looking at the oilers bracing new timbers forward of the buckled plates as a precaution, the water still sloshing around their legs. It wasn't enough water to make the vessel loggy, but that's just how she felt, as if she were becoming a dead weight.

"Pappy, have you checked all compartments?"

He wearily nodded. "I was busy here, but Phelps did the checking. They're all O.K."

"Did he check the holds?"

"He didn't say so, but I assume ..." Garrett stiffened. He looked at me.

I took the ladder on the run, Garrett behind me. We roused all hands to clear away the booms and debris from Number Two. I didn't need a flashlight when I lowered myself down into the cargo manhole. I could hear it behind the cargo battings: the rush of sea water.

Somebody on deck started screeching we were going down. Garrett snapped him into silence. I popped my head up out of the manhole and looked at Garrett. "Tell Ferguson to pump Number Two. It's going to be quite a night, Pappy."

It was. It was a nightmare of wading through water, cursing at the sweating men for more speed. Under the light of flickering lanterns they feverishly set about erecting a wall against a rupture running the entire length of the hold. A makeshift collision mat had been placed over the side to help break the pressure of the seas, but it still required the labor of all hands to stem the flow. Phelps alone was on the bridge, acting as helmsman, and Silva's job was to keep coffee and food coming. All others worked with me, calking, pressing mattresses and cotton waste into place, and shoring with timbers. Stop holes were burned in front of hairline cracks and then plugged, with a prayer they wouldn't skirt the plugs and extend into the fo'c'sle.

It was trying work as the night wore on. Sometimes a section of cofferdam would be completed, the cement in place. Everyone would breathe freely for a few moments; and as if that were the signal, it would crumble as that particular plate twisted or sagged further. Only one thing was in our favor: the storm was lessening its force. We still took an occasional sea over the bow, but the steady pounding had fallen off.

By four in the morning some progress was being made; barely noticeable, but still it was progress. The pumps began holding their own.

It was Garrett who took me by the collar and forced me out of the hold.

"You'll be a dead man by morning, lad, if you don't take a breather. Take an hour or two rest."

I was in no condition to object. I had been bleeding steadily from the opening in my scalp, and it was a case of lying down either in the hold or in my room.

On my way forward I passed Silva carrying coffee and sandwiches to the men. I was too exhausted to look up at him. I had the feeling he had stopped to watch me going toward my room, but beyond reminding myself to lock my door I gave him little thought. You reach a point where nothing matters except sleep.

"What are you doing in here?" I slammed the door shut behind me.

Joyce was sitting at my desk. She pushed the left drawer closed and got up, trying to look unconcerned. "I've been working on the books and thought you might have some expense vouchers in your desk."

She was still a lousy liar.

"Books? In this weather?"

She shrugged. "It's the only thing I have to do to keep my mind off the storm—and the possibility of our going down."

"We're not going down." I moved over to the desk. "Find your vouchers?"

She shook her head. "Another time will do."

"Stick around a minute and I'll get them for you." What the devil had she been up to?

I sat down behind the desk and pulled out the drawer she had just closed. A bottle of brandy was there, half empty. Also my pistol.

I took out the brandy, looked at it. I looked at Joyce. "Care for a drink?"

She went over and studied Sloan's oil painting over the bunk. "No, thank you. Not just now."

"Not from this bottle, eh?"

She wheeled, looking annoyed. "If you think— Oh, don't be ridiculous!"

I took out the pistol and dropped it into my pocket. "Then why don't you want a drink?"

"All right, then, I will."

I shut the drawer without taking the bottle out. "Guess you didn't have time to load the stuff with some of Sloan's pills."

And she hadn't the time. I could tell by her affected nonchalance.

"Don't tell me I've been worrying you lately! The rough and tough Captain Lewandowski being worried by a woman? My, my."

The fact that I *was* worried suddenly made me sore. "How are you making out with your new boy friend?"

A flush crept over her face. "Always ready with a clever word, aren't you, Captain? Well, perhaps there'll come a time when you won't feel at all clever. Now if you'll give me the vouchers I'll leave."

I pulled open another drawer and made a pretense of searching for them. My head was aching and I could hardly keep my eyes open, but I fooled around in the drawer, asking myself some questions: Why beat my brains out worrying about what those two were planning? Was I to be looking behind me every night wondering where Silva was, or sit down to my meals wondering if the next mouthful would be my last? Why not play it cute? It would only be until we reached Frisco. Once in port, both she and Silva would be the first off the gangway and for keeps. I'd see to that.

Give this idea a try, anyway.

"Joyce, I've been doing some thinking lately. Here we are at loggerheads all the time and maybe for no good reason. O.K., I was pretty upset in the past; not built to take certain things, I guess. But it's over and behind us now, and ... well, oh, hell, let's forget them and make a fresh start!"

She blinked at me in disbelief.

"Here's the way I figure it, Joyce. We're partners. We have our best interests in common. If we keep pulling in opposite directions, everything we've worked for may disappear."

"Whose fault would that be? Haven't I, time and again, tried to make you understand that we had everything before us if we wanted it that way?"

I nodded. "You have. Guess it took me a while to see it."

She looked uncertain, as if not quite believing me.

"It's a little silly to keep working against each other, Joyce. I think it's best if we become friends again. We have everything to gain from it, nothing to lose."

"And I told you that right at the beginning, Martin. That's exactly what I told you. It's been you, not me, who's been working against our future." She came over to the desk, the disbelief now gone, replaced by eagerness. "Of *course* it's best if we become friends again. The sensible thing. I'm willing to overlook what's happened and, believe me, that's not easy to do. You've acted miserably toward me. You know you have. Now admit it."

I admitted it. My stomach was turning. She was slopping over at the mere idea that things could be the same again. That's what was making it easy: She was a woman carrying an unquenchable thirst, willing to believe anything for a little relief.

"You *will* be a good boy in the future." She stood beside me, her hand touching my head. It was an effort but I didn't flinch.

"Say you will, now." Her arm slid around my neck. "Say you'll be a good husband, no more foolish arguments."

"Sure thing, Joyce. We'll try to get along."

"Your poor head is a terrible mess, isn't it?" She bent down and pressed her cheek against mine and suddenly laughed. "Martin, dear, did you know I hit you with my shoe when we were together in that sampan? When I saw you lying there, drunk and bloody, I got so mad I took my shoe off and gave you some good ones."

"Rated it, I guess."

"You did, indeed. You acted brutal toward me and I didn't know how to get back at you."

She rubbed her cheek against mine. "Tired, dear?"

"Sure am. But I've got to go below again."

She whispered against my ear, "Martin, I'm glad it can be the same again. I'll wait here."

"I'll be some time, Joyce."

"Don't you *want* me to wait?"

"Sure, but—"

"Then I'll wait. And no buts."

She patted my cheek, straightened, and went over to the bunk. "I'm tuckered out, too. Lord, I really got a fright before when that wave hit us. I thought sure we'd be smashed to pieces."

I got up, wondering if I'd made a bonehead play. Now I'd be spending all my time thinking of ways to keep her out of my hair. Maybe it would have been easier and smarter to slap Silva in irons on some pretext.

"Will you turn the lights out? And hurry back."

I snapped them out, the room falling into darkness. I started to open the door.

"Martin."

"Yeah?"

"We've really forgiven each other, haven't we? I mean we'll get along nicely together again, like we did at the beginning? Like that night on the beach in Chefoo?"

"Sure, you bet." For a million I could never touch her again. Some things are physically impossible.

"Martin, remember the swim?" Her low-throated laugh came through the darkness. "Remember the pebbles under your back?"

Play the game.

"Really hurt, too."

"I'll bet you didn't mind, though."

"Well, no. Guess I didn't. Listen, I have to get below. See you, huh?"

"All right, darling."

I closed the door, went around to the port side and into Garrett's room. I flopped on the bunk and in six seconds flat was sound asleep.

You could feel it in the motion of the ship, the wind dying, the sea beginning to smooth. It brought me wide awake.

Through the ports I saw it was still dark, and debated whether to sleep on or go below to see how things were. I got up finally, put my coat on, and went outside into the passageway.

It was a sixth sense that made me step back into the shadows of the bridge house, out of sight of Silva, who was standing a few feet from Joyce's cabin, looking furtively around as if he couldn't make up his mind about something.

He took one last look aft, saw the decks were still deserted, then ducked down the starboard passageway.

I stood there a moment, puzzled. The only rooms on the starboard side were the storeroom and mine. Assuming Silva was trying to sneak a talk with Joyce, how did he know she was in my room?

The answer came: He didn't!

I broke into a run then, dragging the pistol from my pocket. All I could think of was the darkened room, Silva slipping across the floor with the knife poised, believing the sleeping form to be me, the knife coming down...

It wasn't a scream, more of a raw agonized gasp from Joyce as I burst into the room, my left hand sweeping across the light switch.

Over by my bunk Silva was staring stupidly down at Joyce, the knife clutched in his fat fist. Joyce was up on one elbow, her pale face turned toward Silva, her lips moving, trying to speak. The stain on her white blouse was spreading, like a dark red rose opening its petals.

Silva turned my way, his broad lips quivering, the knife in his hands a smear of blood. "She said ... she said ..." The words stuck in his throat. His mouth opened and closed. Then a crazy look came into his eyes and he came charging across the room at me, the knife coming up.

The bullet caught him right above the bridge of his nose and stopped him dead. His eyes crossed in a funny way, as if he were trying to see what had hit him in the face.

I didn't wait for him to fall. I went over to Joyce. She was still up on one elbow, her face twisting in pain.

"Martin ... Oh, God!"

I pushed her gently back on the bed. "Try not to talk, Joyce. Let me have a look." She gripped my hand as I tried to undo her blouse. "Martin, it went through me.... Oh, God, it went all the way through!"

"Joyce, please. Don't talk."

She pulled me down to her, choking it out. "M-Martin, I told Silva you were in our way. But I really loved you. I wanted something to happen to you but I loved— Oh, God, I can't stand it!"

She lasted almost two hours. Garrett and I worked over her, doing everything possible to hold life in her. We clamped the wound, and when she lost consciousness from loss of blood Garrett tried some crude blood transfusions. To an extent they worked. Once, before dawn, she opened her eyes, with just enough strength to smile up at me.

"You did come back.... What a horrible dream, Martin."

"Joyce, can you drink a little brandy? Just a little?"

She didn't answer. Her smile became fixed. Her eyes lazily closed.

She sighed a little, and that was all.

"So that's it, Pappy. The whole story. You can say I've plenty of guilt in this, that maybe I was the cause of the whole thing. Maybe so. Maybe not. All I know is I didn't kill Sloan. I wanted nobody dead. So I don't intend to play sucker by going to the police with the real story."

Garrett shrugged. "If you feel you're free of guilt, there's nobody to say otherwise."

We were up on the flying bridge, watching the eastern sky brighten the horizon. Ahead of the Trader's bow stretched a peaceful sea, long gentle swells rising and falling.

"It's not so much being free of guilt, Pappy. The law wouldn't say I'm free. But Sloan can't be brought back to life by my playing Rover Boy. Nobody can be brought back. Silva went berserk and *that* is for the record."

Garrett nodded. "That's for the record. And where do you go from here, lad? Your marriage to Joyce makes the Trader yours."

"My first act, Pappy, is making you skipper."

He looked surprised. "And you?"

I leaned over the weatherboard and watched the rim of the distant sky glowing, the promise of fair weather ahead. "Pappy, hulls can be had pretty cheap, almost for the promise to pay. If times get any worse everything would come to a standstill, and I don't think that will happen. When we reach Frisco I'm putting another vessel in service. The Eastern Trader will back it. Later, maybe, I'll get still another."

"Frankly, lad, I don't envy you. But suppose we go below and have a drink on it."

On the way down the ladder I couldn't help thinking of Ezra Sloan, and wishing he were there to have a drink with us.

THE END

Calvin J. Clements was born February 14, 1915 in Jersey City, New Jersey, and attended high school for one year. He became a fireboat pilot in the New York City Fire Department, and retired after 20 years to take up writing. Clements is best known as the author of adventure stories, three novels for Gold Medal Books,  and various movie and TV screenplays, including 39 episodes of Gunsmoke. He died March 11, 1997 in Tarzana, California.

Calvin Clements Bibliography
(1915-1997)

NOVELS:
Satan Takes the Helm (Gold Medal, 1952)
Hell Ship to Kuma (Gold Medal, 1954)
Barge Girl (Gold Medal, 1953)
Dark Night of Love (Popular Library, 1956)

SCREENPLAYS (all TV except where noted):
Wanted: Dead or Alive (1 episode, 1959)
Law of the Plainsman (3 episodes, 1959-60)
Have Gun—Will Travel (1 episode, 1960)
Laramie (1 episode, 1960)
The Detectives (2 episodes, 1960-62)
The Rifleman (10 episodes, 1960-63)
Zane Grey Theater (1 episode, 1961)
The Brothers Brannagan (1 episode, 1961)
Ichabod and Me (1 episode, 1961)
Bachelor Father (1 episode, 1961)
Alfred Hitchcock Presents (1 episode, 1961)
The Greatest Show on Earth (1 episode, 1963)
The Great Adventure (1 episode, 1964)
Daniel Boone (1 episode, 1964)
Gunsmoke (39 episodes, 1964-74)
Wagon Train (5 episodes, 1964-65)
Karen (1 episode, 1965)
Convoy (1 episode, 1965)
Firecreek (movie, 1968)
The Sixth Sense (1 episode, 1972)
Kansas City Bomber (movie, 1972)
Jigsaw (1 episode, 1972)
The F.B.I. (6 episodes, 1973-74)
Dirty Sally (1 episode, 1974)
Attack on Terror: The FBI vs the Ku Klux Klan (TV
    movie, 1975)
How the West Was Won (3 episodes, 1979)

Black Gat Books

Black Gat Books is a new line of mass market paperbacks introduced in 2015 by Stark House Press. New titles appear every other month, featuring the best in crime fiction reprints. Each book is size to 4.25" x 7", just like they used to be, and priced at $9.99. Collect them all.

1 Haven for the Damned
by Harry Whittington
978-1-933586-75-5

2 Eddie's World
by Charlie Stella
978-1-933586-76-2

3 Stranger at Home
by Leigh Brackett
writing as
George Sanders
978-1-933586-78-6

4 The Persian Cat
by John Flagg
978-1933586-90-8

5 Only the Wicked
by Gary Phillips
978-1-933586-93-9

6 Felony Tank
by Malcolm Braly
978-1-933586-91-5

7 The Girl on the Bestseller List
by Vin Packer
978-1-933586-98-4

8 She Got What She Wanted
by Orrie Hitt
978-1-944520-04-5

9 The Woman on the Roof
by Helen Nielsen.
978-1-944520-13-7

10 Angel's Flight
by Lou Cameron
978-1-944520-18-2

11 The Affair of Lady
Westcott's Lost Ruby /
The Case of the Unseen
Assassin by Gary Lovisi
978-1-944520-22-9

12 The Last Notch
by Arnold Hano
978-1-944520-31-1

13 Never Say No to a Killer
by Clifton Adams
978-1-944520-36-6

14 The Men from the Boys
by Ed Lacy
978-1-944520-46-5

15 Frenzy of Evil
by Henry Kane
978-1-944520-53-3

16 You'll Get Yours
by William Ard
978-1-944520-54-0

17 End of the Line
by Dolores &
Bert Hitchens
978-1-9445205-7

18 Frantic
by Noël Calef
978-1-944520-66-3

19 The Hoods Take Over
by Ovid Demaris
978-1-944520-73-1

20 Madball
by Fredric Brown
978-1-944520-74-8

21 Stool Pigeon
by Louis Malley
978-1-944520-81-6

22 The Living End
by Frank Kane
978-1-944520-81-6

23 My Old Man's Badge
by Ferguson Findley
978-1-9445208-78-3

24 Tears Are For Angels
by Paul Connelly
978-1-944520-92-2

25 Two Names for Death
by E. P. Fenwick
978-195147301-3

26 Dead Wrong
by Lorenz Heller
978-1951473-03-7

27 Little Sister
By Robert Martin
978-1951473-07-5

Stark House Press

1315 H Street, Eureka, CA 95501 707-498-3135
griffinskye3@sbcglobal.net   www.starkhousepress.com
Available from your local bookstore or direct from the publisher.

MEET
21 - WOMAN, THEN HER HUSB.
30 - HIRED TO CUT EXPENSES
34.5 - SCREAMING MATCES
34. MORE THAN FILM PLANT
RUST (LIKE TIGER SHARK)
24 - INJURES (SLOAN)
67 - CONF. HIM
76 - PLAYS UP COMMERCE —
CONC ON SHIP
77 - Q
- PEELING PAINT / RUST **
97. "COOLIES"
101- Q
122 - BEATS HER, IN ANGER
IN WHP, C. OR CHEATING
137 - HE STUCK - SHE - IN CONTROL
142 - MINUES/?
174 - WEATHER - TOO MUCH
TO REF, PROBLEM
BUT IN GOOD DETAIL

Made in the USA
Columbia, SC
22 October 2020